ROMANCING THE CROWN

A kingdom holds its breath…a duke comes out of hiding…trial and temptation meet as the search for the missing crown prince of Montebello stretches across the globe!

Meet the major players in this royal mystery…

Duke Maximillian Ryker Sebastiani: The Disenchanted Duke will do anything to help the search for his missing cousin, the crown prince of Montebello. Even give up his precious anonymity…and maybe his heart!

Cara Rivers: Life has taught the bounty hunter to trust no one. Now her destiny rests in the hands of an intriguing man whose very identity is suspect.

King Marcus Sebastiani: His Majesty hopes the criminal his nephew Max seeks will hold the key to finding his missing son and heir.

Kevin Weber, aka Jalil Salim: Is he a petty criminal? Or a threat to the crown of Montebello?

Dear Reader,

They say that March comes in like a lion, and we've got six fabulous books to help you start this month off with a bang. Ruth Langan's popular series, THE LASSITER LAW, continues with *Banning's Woman*. This time it's the Banning sister, a freshman congresswoman, whose life is in danger. And to the rescue… handsome police officer Christopher Banning, who's vowed to get Mary Bren out of a stalker's clutches—and *into* his arms.

ROMANCING THE CROWN continues with Marie Ferrarella's *The Disenchanted Duke,* in which a handsome private investigator— with a strangely royal bearing—engages in a spirited battle with a beautiful bounty hunter to locate the missing crown prince. And in Linda Winstead Jones's *Capturing Cleo,* a wary detective investigating a murder decides to close in on the prime suspect— the dead man's sultry and seductive ex-wife—by pursuing her romantically. Only problem is, where does the investigation end and romance begin? Beverly Bird continues our LONE STAR COUNTRY CLUB series with *In the Line of Fire,* in which a policewoman investigating the country club explosion must team up with an ex-mobster who makes her pulse race in more ways than one. You won't want to miss RaeAnne Thayne's second book in her OUTLAW HARTES miniseries, *Taming Jesse James,* in which reformed bad-boy-turned-sheriff Jesse James Harte puts his life—not to mention his heart—on the line for lovely schoolteacher Sarah MacKenzie. And finally, in *Keeping Caroline* by Vickie Taylor, a tragedy pushes a man back toward the wife he'd left behind—and the child he never knew he had.

Enjoy all of them! And don't forget to come back next month when the excitement continues in Silhouette Intimate Moments.

Yours,

Leslie J. Wainger
Executive Senior Editor

Please address questions and book requests to:
Silhouette Reader Service
U.S.: 3010 Walden Ave., P.O. Box 1325, Buffalo, NY 14269
Canadian: P.O. Box 609, Fort Erie, Ont. L2A 5X3

The Disenchanted Duke
MARIE FERRARELLA

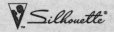

INTIMATE MOMENTS™
Published by Silhouette Books
America's Publisher of Contemporary Romance

Special thanks and acknowledgment are given
to Marie Ferrarella for her contribution
to the ROMANCING THE CROWN series.

To Pat Teal,
with all good wishes for a full recovery,
Love, Marie

 SILHOUETTE BOOKS

ISBN 0-373-27206-5

THE DISENCHANTED DUKE

THE SEBASTIANI FAMILY

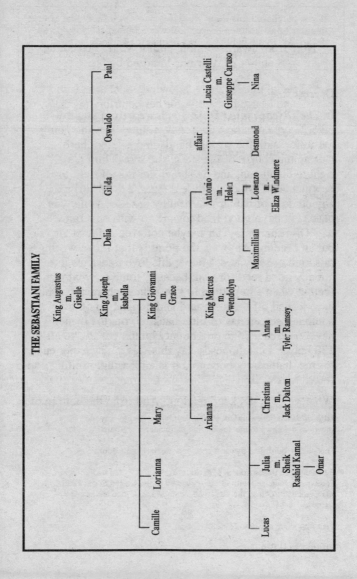

Note from award-winning author Marie Ferrarella,
author of over one hundred books:

Dearest Reader,

In *The Disenchanted Duke* you have before you my
favorite type of story: the feisty, chipper heroine going
toe-to-toe with the strong, handsome, somber hero.
During the course of the story, she shows him it's all
right to be human, and he shows her it's all right to
be vulnerable. Mix in a little danger, a little intrigue,
a good dose of banter and healthy sex, and voilà, you
have (I hope) a good read to curl up with on a rainy
day. Or a sunny day. Or maybe not even a day at all,
but an evening. Anyway, the point is that I love writing
this kind of story and, I hope, this love translates into
a really good read for you, because some of what I'm
feeling when I'm getting to know these characters who
have leaped off the keyboard and popped up on my
computer screen has to filter back to you, the reader. I've
never tackled a duke or a bounty hunter before, so after
130 books, I can honestly say this was a new experience
for me. I sincerely hope that it is a pleasing, exciting one
for you, as well.

Whatever you do, keep reading! And from the bottom of
my heart, I wish you love.

Marie Ferrarella

Chapter 1

"You got a strange call in this morning that you might not want to return."

Max Ryker had just walked into the first-floor office that he maintained in Newport Beach's trendy Fashion Island, a warm check in his pocket and the satisfying rush of a job well done still coursing through his veins. He paused before closing the outer door, puzzled by the enigmatic sentence his grandfather had just greeted him with.

"Well, seeing as how I just wrapped up a case for Lilah Beaumont." He mentioned the name of the most recent Hollywood star who had availed herself of his well-honed investigative services, "if the call is about taking on a new assignment, strange or not, the odds are I'll be returning it."

William Ryker pivoted the wheelchair he'd learned to operate expertly like an extension of the legs that no longer obeyed his command and looked at his grandson. A fortuitous twist of fate had brought Max back into his life nearly sixteen years ago after an absence of almost twenty. It wasn't many men who found themselves learning to become a grandfather to a full-grown man.

For all intents and purposes, he and Max came from two different worlds. But Bill was grateful for the chance to bridge that gap and the years that had come before.

Grateful, too, that even now his handsome, thirty-six-year-old grandson had gone out of his way to find a place for him in his life. Bill spent his days working as Max's all-around man Friday at the detective agency Max had started up several years after he left his birthplace, the tiny kingdom of Montebello, and came to live in Southern California. Felled by a robbery suspect's bullet five years ago and confined to a wheelchair by a shattered vertebra, Bill found that working at the agency gave him the opportunity to use the experience he'd amassed in his years on the L.A. police force.

It made him feel useful, something he knew Max tacitly understood.

"I don't know about that," Bill murmured in response as he moved the large wheels of his chair to the desk where he'd left the carefully written message. His aim was less than perfect, and one of the wheels hit the side of the desk. He cursed quietly, righting his position.

Max watched his grandfather maneuver his wheelchair. He knew better than to get behind Bill and push. A man's pride was a fragile thing and should be respected. Still, it bothered him to see the man struggle.

Max suppressed a sigh. "I wish you'd let me get you a motorized one."

It was familiar ground. They'd covered it more than once before. Bill knew the concern came out of love rather than impatience or a tendency to patronize, so it didn't irritate him. He picked up the phone message, then spun the chair around 180 degrees.

"And I told you I don't need one of those fancy things. How'm I supposed to get my exercise if I sit on one of those metal magic carpets? Besides," he snorted, "the batteries could die while I'm out in the middle of nowhere, then what?"

Max shook his head. Sometimes he thought the Rockies would sooner crumble than his grandfather would change his mind once he'd made it up.

But for argument's sake, he said, "Then you call me on the cell phone you'd have with you and I'd come and get you."

The answer made no impression. "Supposing you're occupied?"

Bill emphasized the last word as if there was only one way that someone as handsome as his six-foot-one grandson could be occupied. He raised and lowered bushy black-and-gray brows in a devilish fashion, wishing with all his heart that he was thirty-six again, too, and whole.

Max grinned fondly at the old man. "For you, Grandpa, I'd always make time."

Funny word, "grandpa," Bill mused. He'd always thought he'd hate the sound of it, that hearing it applied to himself would make him feel old. But he had been separated from both his grandsons by his late daughter, Helen, for so long that all he felt whenever he heard the name was grateful.

"Here." Bill held out the yellow piece of paper he'd written the long telephone number on. The former police sergeant fervently hoped that what was on the piece of paper would not ultimately take the young man out of his life again. Not after he'd waited all this time to have Max come into it.

Max's smile faded just a shade as he read the message. It was just two words: Please call, and a name, followed by a telephone number.

The number was only vaguely familiar, but the name—the name was something else again. The name belonged to a man Max owed his allegiance to. Not as a subject of the man's country, and not even because King Marcus of Montebello was his uncle, but because the monarch of the small country was his friend as well. At times, when he was growing up, Max had felt that Marcus was the only friend he had in a country where he'd never quite fit in, despite his royal ties and family name.

Max's full name was Maximillian Ryker Sebastiani and he was a titled member of the royal ruling house of Montebello, a small, proud country that occupied an island located halfway around the world from the United States. But he'd shed his title and then his last name in what had proved to be a semifutile bid for anonymity. He'd wanted no part of a house that had spawned the likes of his father, Antonio, the dashing, womanizing duke who had warmed countless beds and broken Max's mother's heart long before she died of leukemia.

His mother had died when Max was fourteen, his father when he was eighteen, and his desire to be part of the royal farce, as he saw it, sometime between the two life-shaping events. Although he'd inherited the title of duke when his father died, he refused to use it. Soon after his father's funeral, he'd joined the royal army.

But two years later had found him feeling just as restless, just as displaced as ever. So he'd packed up a few belongings and left his father's country, hoping to find his true destiny somewhere within his mother's homeland.

To his surprise and relief, his grandfather had welcomed him with open arms and put him up in the house where his mother had known happier days. For Max it turned into the homecoming he'd hoped for. After searching for his roots for twenty years, he'd finally found a place for himself.

He'd conceived of the agency six months after his grandfather's fateful encounter with a robbery suspect had landed Bill flat on his back with nothing to look forward to. He'd deliberately chosen the detective agency to give his grandfather's life a purpose. As a bonus, it had given him one, too.

Bill watched his grandson look at the note and could almost hear the wheels turning in the younger man's head. Max had a call to make. He turned his wheelchair around again, heading for the door.

"Open the door for me, boy. I need to get one of those dinky cups of coffee they overcharge you for at the café," Bill told him, referring to the small coffee shop located along the outside perimeter of the eight-floor office building.

Max crossed to the door, opening it. He knew what this was about. Nobody respected space the way his grandfather did. "You don't need to clear out."

Bill spared him a kindly look. "Figure I'll give you some privacy."

Max closed the door after his grandfather and went back to the desk. Taking a seat, he placed the message down on the blotter and studied it for a long, silent moment before he finally picked up the receiver. Blowing out a breath, he pressed the series of numbers that would connect him with the palace. Something akin to a melody resounded as he tapped on the keys.

It took awhile for the connection to kick in. The line, he knew without being told, was a private one which went directly to the king's own offices, circumventing the army of secretaries and go-betweens that were usually encountered when making such calls.

The only person Max had to go through was the King's personal secretary, a gruff old man named Albert who was exceedingly protective of the monarch's time. Only after Max had volunteered the name of his father's last mistress did Albert believe he was who he claimed to be and put him through.

"I would have thought that old bulldog would have died years ago. What is he, eighty?" Max asked when he finally heard his uncle's deep voice say hello on the other end of the line.

"Eighty-two," the king corrected. "And I couldn't get along without him. Maximillian, my boy." There was sincere pleasure in the monarch's deep voice. "How long has it been? Never mind, whatever the time, it has been far too long."

Max knew exactly how long it had been. Though he cared a great deal for his uncle and aunt, and was very fond of his brother Lorenzo, his visits to Montebello were few and very far between.

"Almost eight years since the last visit."

"Eight years," Marcus marveled. Where did time go? It seemed like only yesterday that the boy had gone. "Don't believe in overstaying your welcome, do you, Maximillian?"

Max knew that his uncle's time was far too valuable for Marcus to have called only to shoot the breeze. There was some other reason behind the call.

"Something like that. My grandfather said you called with urgent business." He embellished slightly, but he had a feeling he was on the right track.

"I'm surprised he gave you the message. He was rather evasive about when you'd be in when I told him who I was."

Max smiled to himself. He knew how cantankerous his grandfather could be. A plainspoken man, Bill made it clear that royalty didn't impress him. "You have Albert, I have Grandpa."

"I see your point," Marcus conceded graciously. He would have liked nothing better than an opportunity to catch up with his dashing, nonconformist nephew, but there were more pressing issues at hand. "Well, then, to business. I need a favor."

It was rare that Marcus ever asked for anything. Still, time had taught Max to qualify things and not jump in headfirst, eyes shut. "As long as it doesn't involve returning to Montebello on a permanent basis, you only have to ask."

Marcus paused. When he spoke, there was a detectable sadness in his voice. "Dislike us that much, do you, Maximillian?"

It wasn't the country or his relatives that Max disliked, it was the memory of his father that haunted him.

"I've always been more American than royal, Uncle Marcus, you know that. I never fit in. Too much pomp and circumstance to suit me. Life is to be savored and explored, not sampled through a gilded cage. What's the favor?"

Marcus weighed his words carefully. "It would actually be right up your alley, as you 'Americans' say. I hear you're a private investigator these days."

Max knew that his uncle possessed an extensive network for garnering information, not the least of which was Gage Weston, the nephew of the king of Penwyck. Marcus usually had all the answers to his questions before he ever voiced them aloud.

"Yes, I am."

"Doing well?"

To the untrained ear, it sounded like a typical conversation between a man and the nephew he hadn't seen in years.

"Yes," Max said.

Marcus laughed. "Talkative as ever, I see." And then his voice became audibly more serious. "All right, Maximillian, I need you to track down a Kevin Weber for me. I'm told he recently—" there was a pause as Marcus hunted for the right words "—jumped bail, I believe it is called. He is wanted for crimes committed in a small town in Colorado."

"That's the expression." Max frowned as he wrote down the name. So far, this wasn't making any sense.

"What do you want with a so-called American bail jumper?"

There was another pause, a longer one this time. And then Marcus said, "Nothing is what it seems, Maximillian, but for now, that is all the information you need. Weber has been spotted in a small town in New Mexico. Tacos or Chaos—"

"Taos?" Max suggested, trying not to laugh.

Even now, he could picture his uncle, his stately brow furrowed as he tried to remember. Marcus was the one his mother should have married, the stable, noble older brother, not his far more outgoing, charming younger brother who broke hearts as a way of feeding his own need for adulation and adoration. Max would have gladly called Marcus "father."

"Yes," Marcus declared. "That is the place. I need this Weber brought back to Montebello."

They both knew that Weber was not the man's real name, but because, despite precautions, you never knew who was listening, the alias the man went by in America would suffice. In truth, "Weber" belonged to a group that was as evil as its name: the Brothers of Darkness. It was they whom the king suspected might have something to do with Prince Lucas's disappearance. Ever since the news broke that Lucas had survived the plane crash over the Rockies a year earlier, the royal family had been searching for the long-missing and beloved Prince of Montebello. Ironically "Weber" was wanted for trying to break into the Chambers ranch, the very place Lucas had last been seen. And now that the king's intelligence agency had positively identified Weber as a member of the Brothers, there was no doubt, in the king's

mind anyway, that Weber had not been a mere bur-
glar, but a man on a mission for the Brothers. A mission that might have resulted in the capture of Lucas,
if Weber had had the chance to catch up with him
before he was arrested for breaking and entering. Now
that Weber had jumped his bail, the king's only hope
was that Max would catch up with him before Weber—or any of the Brothers—did.

"When you bring Weber back," the king began,
for the idea that Maximillian would fail to bring the
man to Montebello never entered the king's mind,
"you and I and Tyler will meet. We need to talk.
Extensively. But until then—well, I am afraid that
these lines are not always secure."

No, Max thought, remembering life in the palace,
they were never that. And the lines were not the only
things that weren't secure. You never knew who
might be listening in on a conversation. In Montebello, beneath its clear blue skies and inviting scen-
ery, there was a state of almost constant intrigue,
something he'd never gotten used to or appreciated.
He liked his intrigue in small doses, wrapped in the
cases he handled, not seeping into his personal life.

"I understand. But you have to give me more than
that to work with."

"I'll have Albert send you a fax of the man's pho
tograph."

Max laughed shortly, unable to picture the crusty
old man operating anything more complex than a two-
line telephone. "How long did it take someone to
teach him how to fax?"

"Longer than most people would have been patient
with, but the result is what matters. Now, along with

the photograph, I can give you a more exact location on Weber, but nothing further right now.''

Max nodded to himself. ''Give me what you can.''

Taos, New Mexico, One week later.

As unobtrusively as possible, she checked the small handgun she carried in the holster strapped to the inside of her thigh. Barely the size of a derringer, the weapon contained a clip with a surprising amount of ammunition. It was a specially made gift for her, courtesy of the gunsmith whose family she had once lived with.

There was certainly enough in the clip to bring the bail-jumping scumbag in the motel room just thirty feet away down to his knees. Except that she didn't need him on his knees, she needed him on his feet. On his feet and walking toward the car she had parked out back.

Cara Rivers hadn't had time to scope out the run-down motel where Kevin Weber was holed up, but there didn't seem to be that much to it. There were two sets of stairs, one on either side of the second floor where his room was located.

She figured that if she rushed the front door, she could catch Weber before he had a chance to make his way out the back window. That he had a plan of escape she never doubted. A man on the run didn't take a second-floor room without working out a way to get out of that room if he needed to. He wouldn't simply leap down two stories without having some kind of contingency plan, a way to break his fall.

From everything both the bail bondsman she

worked for and the sheriff of Shady Rock, who she unofficially worked with, had told her, she knew that Kevin Weber wasn't stupid. Quite the contrary, the man was nothing if not crafty. So crafty that she wondered what he'd been doing in the likes of Shady Rock. Luckily, she thought as she made her way slowly up the stairs, she was just as crafty.

If she hadn't been, Cara would have never chosen her present profession, would have never been able to make any sort of a living as a bounty hunter.

Bounty hunting was something she had begun doing shortly after she'd put herself through college and discovered that strict law enforcement, with its binding rules and regulations, just wasn't for her.

Bounty hunting wasn't exactly the kind of vocation most people associated with someone who looked the way she did, but that was the kind of advantage she made full use of. Blond, blue-eyed and delicate-boned at five-four, Cara looked as if her biggest concern in life was how to get her tan even and how long she wanted her bangs to be. Men told secrets to women who looked like her. They let their guards down because they thought her IQ was undoubtedly only slightly higher than her supple bust size. They were always unpleasantly surprised to find out otherwise.

Surprising, too, was the fact that she was as tough as she looked soft. But that had been dictated by not only the life she presently lived, but by the one she had lived through her adolescent years, when she was being passed around from one foster home to another. Being soft meant being hurt. Early on she had learned to depend on only herself. That way, there was never anyone to let her down.

Cautiously she made her way toward Weber's door from the right stairway. She had tailed the man here after putting in more than two weeks of following clues and canvassing the various places he had been known to frequent recently within the Taos area. Weber had been a no-show in all but one of them, and even there, she'd been too late to get the drop on him. She was running out of time.

Wearing a wig with hair down to her waist and a skintight outfit, Cara had planned to proposition Weber and get him into the parking lot. Once there, she'd thought the weapon strapped to her thigh and the handcuffs she kept in her car would do the trick.

But Weber was nowhere to be seen in the seedy, smoky bar. The seat the bartender pointed out where her quarry had been sitting was still warm.

Defeated, she'd sat down at the bar herself and ordered a beer. It was only after she'd hoisted the glass that she noticed there was an empty matchbook carelessly left behind on the table. From the way its edges were bent, Cara figured Weber had used it to pick his teeth.

More important was the imprint on the back. It belonged to a popular, inexpensive chain of motels. Systematically, she'd gone to all of them in the region. As she'd discovered to be par for the course, the one farthest from the bar and the last on her list had turned out to be the right one.

Cara had flashed the photograph she'd gotten from the bail bondsman who signed her checks, showing it to the man at the office. She'd accompanied the photograph with a tearful story involving broken promises and a baby on the way. By the time she was finished, the manager had melted, volunteering that the man she was looking for was staying in Room 218.

A movement on the opposite stairway caught her attention. She saw a tall, somber-faced man walking up the stairs. Dark complexed with dark brown hair and broad shoulders, he could have been a male model in one of those pricey magazines that catered to the upper crust. But the way he had his hand in his pocket alerted her.

There was no doubt in her mind that his hand was covering a handgun.

It was another bounty hunter.

Incensed, Cara would have bet her well-earned reputation on it. She knew a professional when she saw one, even a handsome one. She thought she could make out the glint of steel handcuffs at his waist. Damn it, there was no way he was going to get her man, not after all the woman hours she'd put in tracking him down.

Cara cut the distance between herself and the door to Room 218 in less than a heartbeat. By the time the good-looking stranger approached, she was standing in front of the door in question, blocking his access to it. With a triumphant toss of her head, she knocked on the door.

A moment later, a deep voice from within the room growled ''Yeah?''

''Housekeeping,'' Cara chirped cheerfully, aware that the man at her side was giving her a very suspicious once-over. Probably because she had no uniform or any of the paraphernalia that would tie her to the profession she claimed.

There was movement behind the door. "They did not say anything about there being any housekeeping."

Rather than answer, she announced, "I have fresh towels." Cara saw the stranger look at her empty arms. "You horn in on this and I'll cut your heart out," she hissed.

The next moment, she heard the sound of a window being opened from within the room. She knew what that meant. Her quarry was escaping.

There were tools in her small bag for moments like this, but with no time to extract them and use them on the lock, Cara took the easier, albeit noisier, route. She pulled out her gun, flashing a long length of thigh as she secured her weapon. There was no hesitation on her part. Taking aim, she shot the lock.

Cara swung opened the door in time to see someone leap from the window.

"Stop!" she yelled, knowing it was a completely useless order. Weber was already airborne.

Racing to the window, she saw that her quarry had leaped into a Dumpster located just beneath the window. Damn, how could she have missed that? The Dumpster was filled to overflowing.

The next moment, he scrambled out and hit the ground running. Taking aim, Cara managed to wing him in the shoulder.

Weber screamed a curse in a language she didn't understand and kept running down the alley.

Chapter 2

For a second, Cara debated leaping out of the window into the Dumpster after the fleeing man. It wouldn't be the first time she'd done something crazy and reckless in pursuit of a bail jumper. And she wasn't the type to be deterred by a little dirt, or a pile of garbage as in this case.

Before she could act on her impulse, a strong hand gripped her by the arm, stopping her.

"He's not worth getting hurt over."

She saw Weber get into a car and pull away. Another opportunity gone. Seething, Cara swung around and glared at the man holding on to her. How dare he presume to lecture her? She shrugged him off with an indignant jerk.

"Well, I hope you're satisfied. You just cost me $10,000."

Max frowned at the crazy woman he'd just stopped

from flinging herself out the window. What the hell was wrong with her? Didn't she realize that if she landed wrong, she could easily break her neck or some other part of her body?

Sucking in his breath, he looked down respectfully at the tiny weapon she had in her hand. The one she seemed not to remember she was holding. Right now, the gun was aimed at the part of him that would put a dead halt to his part in propagating the Sebastiani lineage if a stray bullet happened to find its way out of that tiny barrel.

Very carefully, he moved her hand so that the weapon she was holding pointed harmlessly at the floor.

"Look, lady, I'm sorry if your boyfriend ran out on you, but it's not the end of the world—"

"Boyfriend?"

Astonished at the feeble mind that could possibly couple together a worthless creep like Weber with her, Cara temporarily lost her ability to speak. Hiking her skirt up, she holstered her weapon, then pushed the material back into place, aware that the man was watching her every move.

"Eyes back in your head, mister," she ordered. "You think that lowlife's my boyfriend? Are you out of your mind? That was my bounty on the lam, not my booty."

"Bounty?" the man echoed.

"Yes, bounty." If he was trying for innocence, the man was a lousy actor. "Don't say it as if it's some kind of a foreign word to you. That's why you're after him, too, isn't it? To collect the money?" It wasn't a question so much as an accusation. "Well, you can't have him. I spent over two weeks tracking that creep down from Colorado and his tail is mine.''

She was firing words at him like bullets from an automatic weapon and it was all Max could do to hold his own. ''You can claim his tail and whatever other parts of him you want once I'm through with him.''

''Through with him?'' Cara cocked her head and scrutinized the man who had just cost her the reward money she had all but had in hand. On second thought, she reassessed her initial impression of him. He looked too well dressed and pressed to be a bounty hunter. ''Is this some kind of private vendetta?''

Interesting that she should choose those words. He would have thought the same thing, if he hadn't known what he did about the situation. On the surface he knew it would have seemed odd that the ruler of a faraway, proud country like Montebello would even know about, much less be interested in, an American bail jumper like Kevin Weber.

His expression was cool, detached, as he looked at the woman who had temporarily thrown a wrench into his plans. ''I don't see how what this is could be any business of yours.''

Cara called him a few choice names in her head, but kept the words from her lips. There was nothing to be gained by telling him what she thought of him, and Cara had learned to play games well. Whatever it took to win. She needed that money and soon.

''Anything that involves that scum is my business—until I bring him into the county court system and collect the reward. Once I get what's coming to me, you can put your bid in for him.'' Her smile was smug, confident. She was going to nail that runaway son of a bitch and she knew it. She'd been at this trade too long to think about failing now. "I'm sure something can be arranged in, oh, say about fifteen to twenty years."

"Is that the sentence Weber's facing?"

He was getting better at this innocent act, Cara thought, evaluating the very masculine man before her. He made it sound as if he was entirely unfamiliar with Weber's offense.

Cara folded her arms before her. "He is now," she told him, although she knew that the sentence depended entirely on the judge and jury. She'd seen hardened criminals go free and hapless losers incur real jail time. She made what she felt was a safe guess. "I don't see Weber getting any time off for good behavior."

Dragging a hand through her long, silky hair, she sighed. Now that Weber knew there were people closing in on him, he was going to be even harder to track down. But nobody'd ever said this job was going to be easy. It would have bored her if it was.

The man looked at her. "What's the offense?"

She narrowed her eyes, studying the man's face, wondering if he was playing her for a fool for some reason. Could he be that ignorant about Weber and still be after him?

"He's wanted for an attempted break-in at the Chambers' ranch." Cara paused, her eyes washing over the man. "You're not a bounty hunter, are you?"

"I'm a private investigator." He put out his hand to her. "Max Ryker."

"Cara Rivers." She shook his hand and was

pleased that he didn't seem to be afraid of hurting hers. He returned her strong grip. ''Well, Max Ryker, your being in the right place at the wrong time just cost me two weeks' hard work.'' She dropped her hand to her side and went back to looking around the room. The closet had only a couple of changes of clothing and nothing else. ''If you're not after him for the burglary, why are you after him—not that it makes a difference to me as long as you stay out of my way,'' she qualified as she pulled open the night-stand drawer. It was empty.

He skipped over the question, going to her final declaration. ''Afraid I can't do that, Cara. My client wants him brought back to Montebello for offenses committed there.''

That was some tiny country halfway around the world, she thought. It didn't matter. She wasn't about to turn Weber over once she had him.

She didn't bother asking who his client was. If Ryker was on the level about being a private investigator, that information was privileged. It was also irrelevant as far as she was concerned.

''Sorry, but the sheriff of Shady Rock might have a few things to say about that. We'll give Weber back after we're done,'' she promised again, a whimsical smile playing on her lips.

Max looked out the window to the alley where Weber had taken off. Sundown was slowly slipping over the entire region.

''Looks like no one's getting him right now.'' He could leave, but Max believed in getting to know whomever he was up against, and something told him that when he went after Weber, he'd find this woman right behind him—if not in front. "Buy you a drink?"

He had to think she was pretty stupid if he thought she didn't see through that. Oldest trick in the book. And also one that didn't work on her.

"And get me smashed so I can't go after him? Sorry, it doesn't work that way." She led the way out of the claustrophobic room. "I don't get drunk."

Though it was a pointless gesture, he pulled the door closed after them. "Is that because you don't drink, or because alcohol has no effect on you?"

He was laughing at her. She'd seen it before. A big, strong, strapping male who thought because she looked the way she did, she was a pushover. Well, they'd just see who was the pushover, wouldn't they?

"The latter."

Amused, Max arched a brow as he looked at her. "Oh really?"

For two cents she'd wipe that smirk off his face. "Yes, really."

He had a man to track down. But now there was no doubt in Max's mind that when he did go after Weber, this feisty female with the pint-size gun and gargantuan ego would be right there, getting in his way. He couldn't afford to have that happen twice. She'd already cost him Weber tonight and the sooner he caught the man, the sooner he'd get his own answers.

The best way to proceed was to make sure she was out of commission for the necessary time. He figured that wasn't going to prove to be a major problem.

"Suppose I buy you that drink," he suggested, "and see."

Now there was a challenge if she ever heard one.

And one challenge begot another. She looked up at him prettily. "Only if you'll join me."

"Done."

He saw nothing wrong in the bargain. He'd been known to drink more than a few with no ill effects. His time in the Montebellan army had been marked by intense training and even more intense drinking during downtime. There was no doubt in his mind that, given her size and weight, it wouldn't take much to send the sprightly blonde sliding under the table, unconscious and out of the way.

Cara hesitated for a moment over the invitation. As much as she wanted to see his butt fried, she knew that joining this man for a drink or three, or however many it took to get him drunk enough to be out of commission would still sidetrack her and take precious time away from Weber's ultimate capture. God knew she needed the money; she'd given her word to Bridgette that it would be there for her when she needed it.

But she had a sneaking suspicion that this stunning specimen of manhood would get in her way again. And she wasn't entirely sure he was telling her the truth when he claimed not to be a bounty hunter. He might very well be one of those smooth-talking ones, bent on getting her out of the way so he could have sole access to the reward. Phil Stanford, the man she worked for, was not above farming out the work to more than one hunter at a time. All Stanford cared about was getting back the money he'd put up for Weber's bail, not any possible moral violations he might have committed in getting that money and the bail jumper back.

If Ryker was working for Phil, then it was in her best interests to get him out of her way. Now.

"All right, I know this bar about a mile away. The Saint." Her eyes washed over him as if she was taking measure. "You don't have to be one to get in."

There was something about her smile that got under a man's skin, Max thought. It was both innocent and calculating at the same time, as if she had a joke she was keeping under wraps, one that he might or might not be in on. Max gestured toward the darkening parking lot. "Lead the way."

She fully intended to. "I'll drive." It wasn't an offer, it was an assumption.

Model-pretty or not, the woman needed to be taken down a notch. "We'll both drive," he told her. "I'll follow you."

She had her doubts about that, but there was nothing she could say. After all, it made perfect sense for him to want to take his car. But she didn't want to risk losing him. Losing him meant failing to eliminate him as competition.

"See that you keep up," she told him. She knew most men were too full of testosterone to let the challenge fall by the wayside.

Still, she kept an eye on her rearview mirror the entire trip to the bar to make sure he wouldn't suddenly turn around and disappear on her.

Parking in front of the ramshackle building with its bright neon sign of a stick figure complete with a fallen halo, Cara quickly got out of her rented '87 Nissan. She was standing beside the driver's door waiting when Max pulled up. He was driving a sleek, black sports car. The vehicle looked as if it had just rolled out of the factory.

It fit him, she thought, but it was a hell of a car for a private eye, if that's what he actually was.

"Private eye business must pay well," she commented, running a hand along the hood as Max unfolded his long torso from the front seat and got out.

Shutting the door, he flipped a switch. The whiny noise told him the antitheft device had been activated. "Can't complain."

If he was on the level, Cara judged that Ryker had to do business with a very high-class clientele. "If your clients can afford to pay you fees that allow you to drive something like that around, what are you doing going after scum like Weber?"

Max carelessly shrugged his broad shoulders. "Long story."

She raised her eyes up to his in a look calculated to make his knees just a little weaker. It annoyed her that he looked unaffected. "It's going to be a long night," she countered.

We'll see, Max thought, opening the door for her. With any luck, he'd have her sleeping it off within an hour, if not less.

Stepping into the Saint was like stepping into a dimly lit, smoky cavern that had faint, piped-in music and was populated by denizens who were more comfortable frequenting the shadows of the night than moving about in the light of day. He'd seen dozen of places like this in as many towns. It was almost painfully stereotypical as far as bars went. He figured that the people who frequented it didn't care.

The door sighed closed behind him. He saw the

bartender nod in their direction. Or was that hers? Lowering his head so that his mouth was level with her ear, he asked Cara, "Come here often?"

A slight shiver danced over Cara's neck, shimmying down her spine. She kept her eyes forward as she crossed to the bar. She'd passed through here three or four times, always on the trail of a bail jumper. The bartender liked to pass on information, for a fee.

But she wasn't about to give Ryker any details. "Often enough."

He couldn't help wondering what a woman like her would be doing in a place like this. She looked like someone's little sister, in need of protection from the kinds of people he saw lounging at small tables, sitting on bar stools, all building relationships with the nondescript glasses sitting directly before them.

But then, he reminded himself, she did have that peashooter strapped to her thigh.

Max found himself thinking about that thigh in great detail. He curtailed the mental journey.

He would have rather taken a table, but she selected a spot at the bar. "So, what'll you have?"

"Whatever you're having," she replied cheerfully, making herself comfortable on the stool.

"Scotch, neat," he told the bartender. Sitting down next to her, Max glanced at the woman he was trying to temporarily put out of commission. She looked as if she weighed somewhere in the vicinity of a hundred and ten pounds, maybe less. He figured he could easily catch her before she hit the floor. He'd rent a room for her at the nearest motel and deposit her there. Maybe she'd learn her lesson and stay out of his way.

"Make it two," she told the bartender.

Max didn't bother hiding the smile on his lips. This, he promised himself, was going to be interesting.

The smoky blue mirror over the bar reflected his expression, bouncing it back to her. Cara spared him a look. "Something funny, Ryker?"

If he went strictly by looks, not manner, she looked like someone who could sit under a shady tree, sipping a tall, cool glass of lemonade. "You just don't strike me as the scotch type."

She exchanged glances with the bartender, although she was fairly certain that because of the angle of her body, Ryker hadn't seen anything. "I'll let you in on a secret, Ryker." She wrapped her hand around the glass the bartender placed before her. "I don't have a 'type.' I am a unique experience."

Max couldn't help the short laugh. He'd run into confidence before, but not on this scale. "Think a lot of yourself, don't you?"

She'd gone the shy, retiring route and it had gotten her abuse and heartache. Cara tossed her honey-blond hair over her shoulder. "Contrary to the popular hope, the meek don't inherit the earth, Ryker. All they get is the dirt."

She caught him off guard. That was surprisingly harsh. "Meek is one word I wouldn't have thought of when looking at you."

The bartender handed Max his glass. Once the bartender withdrew, Max picked up his drink and touched the rim of his glass to hers. "Here's looking at you, kid."

She smiled, then threw the drink down in a long gulp that had Max staring at her incredulously.

"Humphrey Bogart in *Casablanca.*" She placed her glass down on the counter. "Don't you have any better lines?"

"Actually that was from *Key Largo,*" he informed her. "Common mistake."

Maybe, she thought, *but you just made another one.*

Waving to snag the bartender's attention, she held up two fingers, then turned her attention back to Max. "So, who are you working for?"

Because he knew a silent challenge when it was given, Max downed his drink and offered his empty glass for a refill as well when the bartender approached. As an afterthought, he took out his wallet and peeled off the appropriate amount of money to cover the four drinks, plus a healthy tip. He placed the bills on the counter.

"You know I'm not at liberty to say."

The question was her way of feeling him out to see what kind of effect the drink had on him.

Taking a breath, she downed the second drink. Glass bottom met countertop with a resounding smack. "That's all right, I already know."

Max followed her lead and downed his drink, although he had to admit that he preferred taking in his alcohol at a slower pace. But then, going this route only meant the lovely creature sitting beside him would cease to be a problem that much quicker.

He was amused at her certainty that she knew who he worked for. There was no way she could be privy to his work for his uncle. But for the sake of distracting her from his true goal, he played along.

"You do?"

"Sure. It's Phil."

"Phil," he echoed. The name seemed to resound briefly in his head as he said it.

"Phil," she repeated, holding her glass aloft so that the bartender could see her from the other end. "Phil Stanford."

Damn it, how was she holding all that alcohol so well and where was she putting it? She should have been slipping off her stool by now. These drinks were potent. His eyelids were beginning to feel as if they could easily peel off.

"I don't know who that is."

Maybe he wasn't lying at that. Cara pushed the conversation another notch to see if she'd stumbled across the truth.

"Sure you do. The nasty son of a bitch who doesn't know the meaning of the word 'ethics.' He hired you because he was afraid I couldn't deliver Weber." Which was a prime insult in her book, seeing as how she had always, always gotten her man—or woman—before. "But I still have almost another week before Phil has to forfeit his bail money and I'll have Weber safely locked up long before then. So don't get any ideas."

The ideas he was getting, fueled with two shots of scotch and working on a third, had very little to do with the swarthy man he'd been sent to round up and everything to do with a woman who made him think of warm, moonlit nights and dancing along the banks of a tranquil river. Barefoot.

Max took a deep breath before addressing the glass in his hand again. He wouldn't mind seeing her barefoot. Up to the neck.

"What makes a woman become a bounty hunter?"

He was aware that it took effort for him not to slur the last word.

It wasn't a new question. She'd heard it before. A dozen times.

"Opportunity," she replied mechanically.

It had been that, pure and simple. She'd spent six months on the Denver police force, feeling hemmed in by all the rules she seemed to always be tripping over, when she spotted the ad in the newspaper, of all places, for a bounty hunter. The notion struck her fancy. She already knew she was a good cop, she was just a bad bureaucrat and not much of what the sergeant liked to call a team player. Becoming a bounty hunter seemed to emphasize all the right things for her.

A new song came on the jukebox. Cara perked up just as Max was going to say something to her. She raised her hand. "Shhh, I like this song."

Max found himself reaching for the hand she'd raised, folding his fingers around it.

Surprised, Cara looked at him questioningly.

"Like it enough to dance to it?" he asked.

A faint smile played along her lips. "Are you asking me to dance, or taking a survey?"

He got off his stool still holding her hand. "The former."

"Then yes." Cara slid off her stool.

Holding her hand, he led her to the tiny, dirty space before the jukebox. His legs felt oddly wobbly, but Max ignored the feeling. The desire to hold this woman came out of nowhere and was suddenly far too great to ignore.

Dancing seemed like the best solution.

Chapter 3

Maybe it was just his imagination gone into overdrive, but it felt as if the beautiful bounty hunter he had in his arms was teasing him with her body. She was teasing him without doing anything more than swaying quietly to the throbbing tempo of the song on the jukebox. It was a love song from the days when couples shared a melody they referred to as "their" song and would exchange secret smiles every time it came on the airwaves.

Max didn't know if it was him or the room, but one of them seemed to be spinning. He wasn't sure if he was rooting for him or the room.

Holding Cara's hand within his, he kept it lightly pressed against his chest and looked down at her. Thoughts he couldn't quite grasp hold of were crowding into his head. She was petite, though far from fragile. Even so, Max had a suspicion that she wasn't quite as indestructible as she presented herself. Almost, but not quite.

Maybe if he focused on talking, the spinning would go away.

"So, what else do you like besides love songs from the forties?"

She raised her eyes to his, an enigmatic smile playing on her lips. "Men who don't ask too many questions comes to mind."

He laughed softly. The exotic scent she was wearing seeped into his consciousness, arousing him. "Sorry, occupational habit."

She cocked her head, amused. "I thought detectives were just supposed to detect."

He stopped dancing altogether and just stayed in place, holding her and pretending to move to the music. "They have to ask questions to do that."

Cara nodded. "All right, you're allowed one question," and then she qualified it. "And I'm allowed not to answer it if I don't want to."

Even standing still was beginning to take effort. And it was having no effect on decreasing the velocity of the room.

"Hardly seems fair."

She raised one shoulder and let it drop. "That's life."

She seemed to be swaying more, he thought. Had the tempo gotten faster? "What's a nice girl like you doing in a job like this?"

Her eyes glinted slightly, though her expression never changed. "Making a decent living the fastest way I know how."

Her scent was beginning to swirl around his senses.

He was having difficulty focusing on the conversation instead of wanting her, but he forged on. "Why not try for something less dangerous?"

She shook her head. "That's two questions. You've exceeded your quota."

He took a deep breath, trying to steady himself, telling himself that everything wasn't tilting—the way he could have sworn it was. "It's an off-shoot of the first questions. Call it 1a."

"I'd call you conniving."

He smiled. Or thought he did. It was getting harder and harder to tell.

"I've been called worse." The room was beginning to go at a really dangerous speed. Sweat popped out on his brow. "Is it me, or is it hot in here?"

The look she gave him was purely innocent. "Is that a line?"

"No, that's—" He lost his train of thought, even as he was attempting to reach for it. "Maybe we should sit the rest of this one out."

Placing his hand to her spine, he escorted her from the floor. Max's head was starting to feel as if it weighed a ton. The bar appeared to be much farther away than it had just a moment ago.

Each step back took more and more effort on his part. He found he had to rest his arm across her shoulders just to keep from falling over.

He tried to focus on her face, hoping that would negate or at least balance out the spinning. "What was in those drinks?"

"Just scotch. But the glasses probably don't always get washed properly," she guessed. "Maybe there was something else left over from the last..."

He didn't hear the end of her sentence. The buzzing in his head became too loud.

And then the room around him folded itself up until it became less than a tiny pinprick. The next second, the pinprick had disappeared entirely.

Max thought he was falling, but that might have been his imagination.

Everything stopped.

Nothing looked familiar.

Max had absolutely no idea where he was, only that his head was killing him and the effort to open his eyes cost him dearly. Each lid felt as if it was glued in place and had to be pried open.

When it was, he found the immediate area encased in a milky shroud. Repeated blinking finally made the shroud disappear.

He'd had hangovers in his time, royal ones if he could be forgiven the pun, and he'd never felt like this before. Neither had he passed out on three drinks before, no matter how potent they'd been.

Just what the hell had happened, and how did he get here, wherever "here" was?

He smelled a proverbial rat. A honey-blonde one with gray-blue eyes, fantastic legs and one hell of a well-shaped butt.

Holding on to the wall beside him, he sat up. Max had to really concentrate to keep the world from tilting over on its side. Only when it was in its rightful place did he finally try to take in his surroundings.

He was in a small area that appeared to be a storage room of some kind. There were broken chairs tucked away in one corner beside unopened cases of liquor.

He realized that he'd been lying on a cot that smelled of beer and various other things, some of which were hard to place, others far too easily identified. He hadn't been the first to sleep on it.

He pressed a hand to his stomach, willing himself not to throw up.

Rising on shaky legs, he made his way over to the closed door and tried it.

To his surprise, the knob turned. He wasn't locked in. Opening the door, Max discovered that he was inside the bar he'd come to with Cara. Last night, if the thin beams of sun that were pushing their way through the partially closed slats at the window were any indication of the time.

Like so many things, the room had looked a lot better in semidarkness. There were dust motes everywhere he looked.

"Anybody here?" he called out.

No one answered.

Gingerly he touched the back of his head, looking for telltale knots that would have indicated his getting hit, which would have explained his sudden passage into darkness.

There were none. No one had hit him in the head to eliminate his presence on the scene.

The odd taste in his mouth told him that scotch hadn't been the only thing he'd ingested last night.

She'd drugged him.

Somehow, when he hadn't been looking, the sharp-tongued bounty hunter with the killer body had slipped something into his drink and drugged him.

Why?

The most obvious reason, he decided, struggling to

curb his anger at being duped like some kind of novice, was that she thought he was a threat to her getting the bounty on Weber.

He heard a noise to his left and immediately reached for the weapon he always kept strapped around his ankle. It wasn't there.

The woman must have taken it, he thought, cursing under his breath. Why should that surprise him?

Wary, Max grabbed a bottle from the counter behind the bar and held it by its neck, ready to smash the bottom off on the bar and use the jagged portion as a weapon at a moment's notice.

"You break that, you pay for it," the man who had tended bar last night told him, coming into the room. He set down the broom and dustpan he was carrying and scratched his thin, concave chest. A cigarette butt hung out of the corner of his mouth as if it was permanently fixed there. The bartender indicated the other bottles behind Max. "You might want to use something less expensive."

Annoyed, Max put the bottle back down on the bar. "Where is she?"

The man coughed before finally asking, "Who?"

Impatience clawed at Max as he struggled to clear his head. It still felt as if all his thoughts were under water.

"The woman I was in here with last night. And before you tell me that you don't know who I'm talking about, I saw the way you looked at her. Like you'd already met. If you didn't know her, you wouldn't have put me in your back room to sleep it off."

The bartender laughed. It sounded more like a

cackle and was followed up by a hacking cough. "I don't know her. Not in any real sense of the word. She's been here a few times and she gave me fifty bucks to let you sack out in the back room." He picked up the broom again and began sweeping half-heartedly. "Would've given me ten more if the lock on the door worked, but it's busted, just my luck."

Max didn't know if he was buying into this, but the buzz in his head was making it hard to think. "So you don't know her."

The man paused again, his expression wistful beneath the day old stubble. "No, but I'd sure like to. Don't meet many of those in my line of work—fiery, not used up," he clarified, then gestured around the establishment. "'Case you hadn't noticed, this isn't exactly an upscale club."

Max didn't bother commenting. He needed answers and if he wasn't going to get them from this character who was little more than one step removed from a barfly himself, he had to fall back on a tried-and-true method. "Got a phone around here?"

The bartender reached behind the bar and brought out an old-fashioned, stark black dial-up telephone straight out of the last century. He placed it on the bar in front of Max.

"But it'll cost you," he said as Max reached for the telephone.

Digging into his pocket, Max pulled out a bill, glanced at it to see the denomination and slapped it down on the counter. Pulling the telephone over, Max dialed his office number back in Newport Beach. Three rings later, he heard his grandfather pick up and give the name of the agency.

"Hi, it's Max," he said into the receiver. He talked quickly, before his grandfather could ask any questions. "I need you to look someone up for me. Cara Rivers. Get me everything you can find: driver's license number, address, priors if there are any, everything," he emphasized again.

"What state am I looking in?" Bill asked, knowing better than to assume anything. Max got around.

Max paused, thinking, trying to pluck facts out of the murky sea that still surrounded his brain. Concentrating, he remembered the woman mentioning something about Shady Rock, Colorado. Maybe that was her point of origin. It was worth a try.

"Colorado." He saw the bartender looking his way. The man made no effort not to look as if he was listening. "Start with a place named Shady Rock."

"Shady Rock, huh?" Bill chuckled. "That's almost as good as Truth or Consequences, New Mexico, or that other place, Hot Coffee."

Max was not in the mood to see the humor in anything, least of all his condition. He was supposed to be able to see through people like Cara Rivers. And most of all, he wasn't supposed to get himself drugged.

"Almost," he agreed. Covering the receiver as he heard his grandfather begin to slowly type on the computer keyboard, Max looked at the bartender. "Got any coffee around here?"

He knew that this was going to take more than a little while. Though he liked to keep on top of the latest technology, his grandfather's idea of typing fast amounted to three words a minute. Tops.

The bartender jerked a thumb toward the small table that was set up against the back wall. A coffee-maker, its pot half empty, was standing there. "Yeah, but it'll cost you."

Way ahead of the man, Max had already produced another five-dollar bill and placed it next to its mate on the bar.

Cara tried not to dwell on the man she'd left drugged in the bar. She knew it went with the territory but she couldn't help feeling guilty, even though she'd slipped the bartender fifty bucks to let Ryker sleep it off in the back room. She forced her thoughts back on her job.

It amazed Cara how the simplest things often tripped people up.

Using credit cards had become an established way of life. People did it without a second thought, not realizing that they were simultaneously generating a paper trail as they paid for their entertainment, or their shoes or their gas.

Weber might be able to do without the entertainment or the shoes, but the gas, she was betting, since he was driving a car in his getaway attempt, was another story.

With her cell phone and her portable fax machine, along with several other state-of-the-art items stashed in the trunk of her car, Cara had managed to track Weber down via the activity on his credit card.

It helped having connections in the right places, she thought with a smile as she looked at the latest reported transaction.

Weber had purchased not only gas, but a burrito

and a giant-size soft drink at a convenience store on highway 25. It was only fifteen miles away.

Putting pedal to the metal, she was there faster than the law would have smiled upon, the worn photograph of Kevin Weber she'd been showing around sitting on the passenger side beside her.

Screeching to a halt next to the small, squat convenience building, its paint peeling away under the unrelenting sun, Cara grabbed the photograph and dashed inside the store.

The temperature in the interior was only marginally cooler than it was outside. The air felt almost thick as she crossed to the counter. The man behind it looked as if he was ready to wilt.

Cara held up the photograph. "Hi, I'm wondering if you've seen this man in the last few hours?"

The man took only a couple of seconds to study the photograph. The other minute and a half were spent studying her.

"He did and Weber's heading north. My guess is that he might be working his way to Canada."

The clerk in front of her nodded in affirmation.

For the first time, Cara fully understood what was meant when someone said they could have been knocked over by a feather.

That voice could only belong to—

She swung around, her eyes wide, her mind racing. She knew who she was going to see even before she looked at him. Max Ryker.

Her mouth went dry. "You're better than I thought you were."

"And you're more underhanded than I gave you credit for." Taking her by the arm, he pulled her aside. He saw the way the man behind the counter was looking at them, his hand hovering over the telephone receiver. "Just a family spat, mister. If you don't want any trouble, just go about your business," Max told the barrel-chested man. His smile faded the moment he had her a safe distance away from her would-be protector. "What the hell did you put in my drink?"

Cara raised her chin. She'd never reacted well to being questioned. Her eyes swept over him. He looked none the worse for wear. The sleepy look in his eyes gave him a sexy appearance from where she stood.

"Nothing fatal."

He snorted. "Obviously." As she began to pull away, his grip on her upper arm tightened. "I don't appreciate being drugged and then dumped."

She looked at him indignantly. "I paid the bartender fifty dollars to let you sleep it off on a bed in the back room."

"It was a cot and it wasn't worth even fifty cents and change," he informed her. But where he'd slept wasn't the issue. What he'd had was. "Now, what the hell did you put in my drink—the truth," he warned.

"Clonazepam." She gave him the generic name. "It puts you out, that's all."

Max was familiar with the drug. It had made the rounds as everything from a tranquilizer to a sleeping pill to a recreational drug for what he deemed to be the mentally arrested, but predominantly was prescribed for seizures.

He arched a brow, looking at her, trying to make

a judgment call that was right for a change when it came to her.

"Yours?"

Cara shook her head. She didn't believe in taking anything more powerful than aspirin, and then only under extreme conditions.

"I know this pharmacist who isn't exactly always on the straight and narrow."

The man was only one of an arsenal of people she'd compiled over her lifetime, people who she turned to whenever she needed a favor that didn't exactly fall within the proper lines smiled upon by society. She figured it was her due, after all the time she'd spent being passed from one house to another, trudging from one closed-clique class to the next over the process of transplantation.

"You wake up a little out of focus," she told him, "a little sluggish, maybe with a fuzzy coating on your tongue, but with no harm done."

If that was a "little" out of focus, then he was Santa Claus's helper. He narrowed his eyes, looking directly at her.

"No harm done—except that you took off."

She shrugged nonchalantly, wishing he'd release her. "Hey, it was just one of those things."

"Don't get cute with me, Rivers. I don't appreciate being drugged and abandoned."

At his raised tone, her own temper flared. "And I don't appreciate being aced out of ten thousand dollars or strong-armed by a bully." This time, she pulled harder against his grip.

Frowning, he released her. "Nobody's strong-arming you."

"Oh, no?" She rubbed her arm to get the circulation going. The man had one hell of an iron grip. "Then what do you call insisting on taking my bail jumper to Outer Slobovia?"

"That's Montebello," he informed her, struggling not to allow the corners of his mouth to curve.

He could almost see the fire leaping in her eyes. Though he was annoyed as hell about her costing him Weber, not to mention time, he had to admit there was something appealing about the way lightning bolts all but came shooting from every part of her.

"And we have jurisdiction," he pointed out. "The U.S. and Montebello have had a mutual extradition treaty for some time now."

"We?" she echoed. She thought she'd heard an accent of some sort. Where the hell was this place he claimed to be from? "Are you a Montebellian?"

"Montebellan," Max corrected. "And that 'we' was just a figure of speech." He didn't want to tell her more than he absolutely had to, and certainly not that he was a duke. The last thing he wanted was annoying attention thrown his way. For some people, anything that had to do with a royal family—and it didn't matter which one—was exciting. "But in any case, Weber's going there when I get him."

She begged to differ with his well-laid plans. "No, he's going to Shady Rock when *I* get him."

Max blew out a breath. "You're going to be a royal pain in the posterior about this, aren't you?"

She smiled sweetly at him. "Until I get my way, you might say that, yes."

He had a feeling that she would cost him every time he got close to Weber. He didn't need any more slipups. Time was money and he wasn't making any on this venture. This was a favor to his uncle. "All right, what do you say we team up?"

It was absolutely the last thing she'd expected him to say—unless he wasn't on the level.

"Team up?"

"Yes, work together to get him."

Cara looked at him suspiciously. Not that she was buying into this for a minute. "And then what?"

"And then we'll work it out."

Just as she'd thought. He was being evasive. Which meant that he didn't want to tell her. Which meant, in turn, that he intended to shaft her.

She shook her head. "And then we bring him to the sheriff of Shady Rock. The office is closer than wherever the hell Montebello is."

"It's an island near Cyprus," he told her automatically. Max couldn't argue about Colorado being closer and he didn't want to waste time arguing about any of the rest of it, either. Every minute that went by, Weber was getting farther and farther away. "Okay." He put out his hand.

Taking his hand in hers, Cara shook it as she looked up at him. "All right, then it's a deal."

"A deal," he echoed.

Her smile never wavered.

She didn't trust him any farther than she could throw him.

Chapter 4

Separating their hands, she dropped hers to her sides. "So now what, 'partner'?"

Max studied her, wishing he knew what was going on in that attractive head of hers. He always liked to know which way the wind was blowing before he set sail. His gut instinct was that, despite the so-called truce between them, he was in danger of standing right in the path of a full-scale gale.

"Why do I get the feeling that you think that's a dirty word?"

Her expression couldn't have been more innocent than if it had been on the face of an angel in a Renaissance painting.

"Interpretation, like beauty, is in the eye—or ear—of the beholder, Ryker. I'm just asking a simple question. You're the one who wanted the partnership."

That was like saying he wanted to play with a basket full of snakes. "Wanted might not be the right word here, but in any case, it's the expedient thing to do, seeing as how we both want Weber and we seem to keep getting in each other's way."

Her eyes narrowed. The innocent expression evaporated. "None of which would happen if *you'd* get out of *my* way."

About to answer her, Max noticed that the convenience store clerk was unabashedly watching them and all but hanging over the counter. "Something I can do for you, mister?"

The young man grinned broadly at them, completely missing the implication. "Hey, man, you're doing it. We don't get much entertainment around here and my satellite dish is busted. Don't know when I can get it fixed. This is the most fun I've had in weeks."

Max took hold of Cara's arm. "Let's take this outside."

She shrugged him off. "I can walk on my own."

"Then walk," he said, holding the door open for her.

Miffed, she walked by him, calling him names under her breath that his ancestors might have taken exception to.

"Spoilsport," the clerk muttered, returning to his copy of a much folded Victoria's Secret catalog.

Max stopped on the sun-rotted wooden porch. "When I got here, just a few minutes ahead of you," Max added the piece of information before she could ask, "the clerk told me Weber had driven off heading north."

Still, that didn't explain the leap on Ryker's part.

"What makes you think Canada? There's an awful lot of territory between here and there, a whole battalion of cities and states."

He shrugged. "Just a guess. It seems to me that a man with two people coming after him from different directions might just want to get out of the country."

That had a germ of truth in it, she grudgingly admitted to herself. But there was still a flaw. "Mexico's closer."

"Yes, but he's heading north. Last time I checked, Mexico was south."

"Maybe he's trying to confuse us by taking a roundabout route."

Max paused. She had a point. "All right, but while we're standing here, talking, he's out there, driving." He indicated the highway. "Let's just follow the road and see where it leads."

Straight to trouble was her guess, but she kept to herself.

"Fine," Cara murmured. "I'll ride point."

"Good." He started to turn to go to his car and realized that she wasn't following. Turning around, Max saw Cara hurrying to her vehicle. She got in before he had a chance to say a word. The car revved up and was heading up the road in less time than it took to process the image.

The woman was a loose cannon.

She had every intention of leaving him in the dust, Max thought with a shake of his head. He'd had a feeling she wouldn't stick to her end of the bargain. Which was exactly why he'd planted a small homing device, no larger than a spot of lint, on her back as he'd put his hand against her shoulder and escorted her from the store. Shrugging him off hadn't dislodged it. Once she took off her clothes, of course, she'd notice it, but for the time being, he was assured that she couldn't get too far away from him.

Cara Rivers drove like a maniac, he thought, after starting his car and getting on the road. The road stretched out before him and she was nowhere in sight.

Except on the screen of his monitor.

A smile curved his mouth. Max took the jacket he'd purposely thrown over the tracking device on the passenger seat of his car and tossed the garment over his shoulder into the back. Rivers was heading due north, just the way she expected Weber to be going.

Why bother losing him if she meant to go in the direction they'd already agreed on? It didn't make any sense to him, but then, he thought with an inward, patient sigh, neither did the woman.

He watched the blip on his monitor and drove due north.

Twilight was beginning to paint the lonely landscape with long, broad strokes when he caught up with her. It wasn't through any fancy driving on his part, but a slowdown on hers. More specifically, a complete stop. Her vehicle apparently had died.

She was on the side of the road, circling the dormant car and yelling at it. He couldn't quite make out what she was saying, but he had a feeling that he was better off that way. The angry expression on her face was enough to send a lesser man running for cover.

Slowing down, Max stuck his head out the window,

a mildly amused, mildly curious expression on his face. "Something wrong?"

Cara was angry enough to spit. There was no way to avoid throwing her lot in with this man now. Worse, she needed him. The next town was too far up the road for her to walk to in the dark on her own.

She hated the dark.

"Yes, something's wrong." For good measure, because she was so furious, she kicked one of the tires. "Bargain rentals rent cars that should have been sent off to the glue factory."

"I think that's supposed to be horses that go to the glue factory," he corrected, not bothering to hide his amusement.

"Not in this case." She snorted. "I would have been better off with a horse. At least with a horse if you feed it and take care of it, it'll take you where you want to go."

"Not in my experience," Max muttered.

He wasn't much for horseback riding, despite the fact that riding to the hunt was supposed to be the sport of kings. But he could easily picture her on the back of a horse. A purebred stallion. Black as the night to contrast with her fair skin.

An image of her riding bareback in the fine old tradition of Lady Godiva suddenly flashed through his brain.

With a start, Max jerked himself to attention. "What seems to be the trouble? With the car," he added, looking at her pointedly as he got out of his vehicle.

Max walked over to her and took a cursory look beneath the hood. There was hardly enough light left to make out the separate parts, much less what was wrong.

Her frowned deepened. There was no point in wasting time tinkering with it. "The distributor cap is burned through."

That was far more specific than he'd ever gotten with a car. He knew enough to keep the fluid levels up, the oil new and jumper cables in his trunk. "And you know this how?"

"I lived with a mechanic for a while."

He looked at her. "Lover?"

She thought of Roy Anderson, potbelly, booming laugh and perpetual grease on his hands. His wife had been a short-order cook in the diner next to his repair shop. One of the many homes she'd passed through in her life in the system.

Roy was roughly forty years her senior and basically a decent guy, but she laughed at the thought of his being anyone's lover, even his wife's.

"Hardly."

Max was tempted to ask her to elaborate, but she didn't look inclined and it was none of his business. He only figured on getting as personal as was necessary with her in order to capture Weber.

"Well, since you're so sure, there's nothing much to be done here." He opened the door to the passenger side. "Hop in. We can call for towing from that town just up ahead."

She'd already seen the faint lights being turned on in the town down the road. Tiny pinpricks against the horizon. They'd been the only thing sustaining her, even though there didn't seem to be enough lights on to properly accommodate the top of a moderate-size birthday cake.

She frowned. She knew towns like that. Small, terminal things where people's souls shriveled up, yearning for something better. Mechanics were not always on hand. Took talent to fix things, make them right. People with talent moved on to where the pay was better, the life more exciting.

"Don't count on it."

"Now aren't you glad I came along?"

She ignored the annoyingly cheery note in his voice. Turning her back to Ryker, she popped her trunk. There was no way she was leaving her equipment behind.

"Otherwise," he was saying, watching her, "it might just be you and the coyotes before long."

The thought was far from thrilling, especially given the way she felt about the dark, a feeling that dated back to the time she was eight and had lived with a minister and his wife who never raised a hand to her, but believed that leaving her in a locked closet for hours would make her submissive to their authority and save her immortal soul.

Cara looked at Ryker and wondered just how much better off she was with this man, who professed to want a partnership with her, than the coyotes. At least with the coyotes, you were aware of the immediate danger.

Leaning into the trunk, she took out the portable fax machine and her notebook computer. She stopped to take her oversize purse out of the front seat along with her shapeless overnight bag and then, arms loaded, trudged over to his car.

"Pop your hood."

Max moved to take something from her, but she pulled back. She was being territorial. Why didn't that surprise him?

"Is that anything like ring my chimes?"

"The car's hood," Cara said from between clenched teeth. The grin on his face was beginning to annoy her immensely. More annoying still was the way his grin made her feel. As if she were a ball of yarn about to tumble down a hill, in imminent danger of unraveling.

He popped the hood as she asked, and Cara placed her things inside the trunk, taking care to secure them as best she could. Rounding the back, she came up to the passenger side and slid in. She hit her feet against something on the floor. Curious, she bent over and picked up the device he had only moments earlier pushed to the floor when he'd seen her.

Her eyes narrowed as she looked at the rectangular object. "What's this?"

He always felt that using the truth as far as it could go was easier than inventing lies from start to finish. He kept his face forward as he started the car. "A tracking device."

Cara examined the lit screen. The cursor was dormant. "Doesn't seem to be tracking anything."

"It's not." Reaching over, he pressed the button and shut it off. The screen went blank. "Got everything you need?"

She traveled light. Her requirements were few. "Except for Weber."

He nodded, taking the car back on the road. "We'll get him, too."

We.

It sounded odd, hearing the pronoun applied to her. She'd never really been part of "we" before. Oh, occasionally the word was bandied about in reference to her within the family she was currently staying with. But no one really meant it. She was Cara and they were "we." If the two mixed, it was only for the moment.

Reality was always waiting for her around the bend. A new family, a fresh separation. She learned to rely only on herself. Cut down on the people to blame as well.

Cara raised her chin, slanting a glance at him. "I don't know about 'we' catching him, but I know *I* will."

"Certainly not a shy, shrinking violet, are you?"

But she had been, more than once. And learned the hard way that selling her soul just for a pat on the head, a hug, a kind word, was selling herself far too short.

"Shrinking violets get their roots pulled up, they get stuck in a vase, then tossed out when they're no longer pretty."

The road ahead was flat, with no headlights coming at Max from the opposite side. He spared her a long look. She made it sound personal. Had she been dumped by a lover? he wondered.

If she had, it would have been because of that razor-sharp tongue of hers, not because her looks had anything to do with it. As far as that went, the woman was a keeper. He bet she'd just love to hear that.

"Sounds as if you've got firsthand knowledge about that."

Cara absolutely hated being analyzed. "Maybe you should hang out a shingle and go into the head shrinking business instead of tailing people other people are after."

He smiled, more to himself than at Cara. "I've had enough career changes for the time being."

She pretended to raise a brow in surprise. "You were something else before you made a habit of getting in other people's way?"

Max thought of life in the palace. If he'd followed in the footsteps of his father, he would have learned how to look down on people and use them to his own advantage. That life had never been for him, even though he'd been trained for it from the day he was born.

"I ran a charm school," Max said sarcastically. He glanced at her again before looking back at the lonely road. "You might have benefited from it."

Cara crossed her arms before her, sitting back in the seat. She promised herself that at the first opportunity, she was going to ditch him again. All she needed was to catch him off guard. She wouldn't even need his car keys, she knew how to hot-wire just about any vehicle. By the time he thought to call the police, she'd be gone and renting another car.

"I really doubt there's anything you could teach me."

Some very personal things, completely unrelated to the situation, came to mind. Max hadn't realized that his mouth had curved into a smile. "You'd be surprised."

"Yes," she said pointedly, "I would be."

The conversation was veering into territory he felt

it was best not to enter. He was having enough stray thoughts about the woman at his side as it was. Max nodded at the lights of the town up ahead. "Let's see if we can find someone to tow your car."

"It's not mine," she reminded him. "I just rented it."

Something told him that the woman didn't allow herself to get too attached to anything. Seeing as how Rivers was on the trail of a bounty, she was traveling incredibly light. Other than her equipment, all she had with her was an oversize purse and what looked like a duffel bag that had seen better days. There was only so much it could hold.

"Then I guess it's the rental agency's problem."

"Guess so," she murmured.

"By the way, you have something of mine."

She braced herself for a trite line. "Oh?"

"My gun. I had one when you left me in that poor excuse for a bar last night. I didn't have it when I woke up. I'd like it back."

Pressing her lips together, she opened her purse and took out the weapon she had lifted. It made a good backup gun. Not saying a word, she placed it on the dashboard between them.

"Thanks." Taking it, Max leaned forward and slipped it into his waistband at the small of his back. He could put it back in its holster once they got into town.

The town they pulled into looked hardly bigger than a truck stop. There were a handful of streets with stores scattered about and a flock of houses just beyond that. Old, weather-beaten houses that had been baking in the sun for a long time, sea lions turning up their faces to the sky.

It didn't look too promising. "I doubt if the rental agency where I got the car has even heard of—Buford," Cara read the town's name on the sign as they drove past it.

He doubted if anyone except for the people who made maps had heard of Buford. "Maybe not, but it's still their problem."

Frustration chewed away at her. Not having a car seriously cut into her independence. "No, it's mine. How am I supposed to get around?"

"Seems to me that you *are* getting around." Max nodded at the car they were in. "It makes combining our efforts a lot simpler."

He didn't intend to combine their efforts, she thought, he intended to use her efforts to secure what he felt was *his* man. *Not going to happen.* Somehow, someway, she was going to make sure that she had first claim. She couldn't afford not to. Literally.

Shifting, she peered out through the windshield. "Speaking of simple, do you think this lovely little town has a hotel?"

Hotels invited a higher clientele than he guessed usually passed through Buford, New Mexico.

"More likely a motel or a motor inn, if anything." He glanced at her, making a judgment call. "Probably not what you're used to."

She laughed softly, thinking of some of the places she'd been in. In foster care all of her life, she'd run away several times when the family she was with had made life unbearable for her. She'd also stayed with some very nice people—people she hadn't allowed herself to grow attached to because there was always a separation waiting for her in the wings.

But the other families were the ones that had left the deepest impression on her, though she pretended, even with herself, that they hadn't.

It was while living with one of the latter, a family named Henderson whose older son had thought that having her stay with them entitled him to gaining access to her body whenever he felt the need, that she had learned how to make do on next to nothing and live by her wits on the street. She'd celebrated her eighteenth birthday living in a discarded refrigerator box beneath a bridge in Denver, Colorado.

Her smile was enigmatic. "You have no idea what I'm used to."

There were scars there, Max suddenly realized. His grandfather had only given him a quick summary of Cara Rivers, Bounty Hunter. But Cara Rivers, the woman, and the person who went into forming that woman, was something that had been left out.

At the time, he hadn't thought it was necessary for him to know.

Now he wasn't so sure.

"Maybe you'll tell me what you're used to over dinner," he suggested.

She looked at him and slowly, her lips peeled back into a smile. It was a line. She knew all about lines—and what was at the end of them.

"Yeah, I can see you running a charm school all right," she quipped. "But you can save your breath, Ryker. It's wasted on me."

His smile matched hers and made her all the more

wary because she couldn't read what was behind it. "I'll be the judge of that."

"You can be anything you want, but I've had my shots against pretty boys." The Henderson's son, Ted, had been almost too beautiful for words. He'd used his looks to his advantage like a skilled swordsman wielded a weapon. She'd been flattered that anyone as good-looking as Ted would pay attention to her. Until she'd realized what he actually wanted.

Max had been called a lot of things in his time, but pretty boy wasn't one of them. And when she said it, the connotation was far from flattering.

"Maybe you're putting me in a category where I don't belong," he told her.

"I'll be the judge of that," she said, throwing his words back at him.

There was no point in sparring this way. He nodded at the obligatory diner that stood like a tarnished, elongated silver can on the edge of the road. "Think the food here is decent?"

She sincerely doubted it. But since it appeared to be the only place in town to serve food and they needed to eat, the point was moot.

"Does the fact that it's such a small town give you a clue?" she asked him.

He wondered if she always saw the glass as half empty, or if this was a part she was playing for his benefit, the reason behind it being something he wasn't allowed access to yet.

"We could drive to the next town," he offered.

She had no idea how far that might be and it was already nightfall. Now that she thought back, she hadn't eaten since around one. That had been a burger and fries as she had driven to her latest Weber sighting. A large container of coffee had been breakfast.

"We're here, we might as well give it a try. It might surprise us."

"Always up for a pleasant surprise," he told her, pulling up next to a dusty blue pickup truck.

The food turned out to be tolerable, though nothing Cara would have wanted to repeat on a regular basis. And the waitress was talkative enough. She looked at the photograph Cara gave her in between ongoing tirades about the condition of her tired feet.

Studying the man's face, the orange-haired woman nodded as she refilled their coffee cups.

"Yeah, I seen him. Not much of a tipper," she said regretfully. She looked around at her clientele. The diner was only one-third full. Cara was the only other woman in the place. "You get used to that kind of thing around here."

Cara tucked away the photograph. "How long ago did he leave?"

"From here?" The waitress considered. "About two hours ago. Looked like he was in a hurry."

Listening, Max took a sip of the coffee. It only got worse with time, but it was hot and black and for now that was enough. "Got a mechanic?"

"We've got Luther, but he's away on vacation." She grinned their way. "Likes to go fishing this time of year."

Well, that was one strike, Cara thought. "How about a hotel?"

The waitress shook her head. A man at the end of the counter waved to get her attention. She waved back. "Nope, don't have one of those. But there's a motel a few miles up the road. They should have a vacancy." She chuckled. "Hell, they always got a vacancy." Coffeepot in hand, she began to retreat to the counter and the customer. "Make sure they give you clean sheets."

"This place just keeps getting better and better," Cara murmured to Max after the woman left.

He thought of the time he'd bummed around Europe before coming to his senses and heading out to where his grandfather lived.

"I've been in worse."

She looked at him and sincerely doubted it.

Chapter 5

She'd had a bad feeling the moment she saw the so-called motel.

Single story, the motel had rooms that were all connected to one another, fashioning a semicircle around a courtyard that had a dry, decaying fountain in the middle surrounded by dead, brown grass and dirt.

Calling the motel run-down would have been kind, but in addition, the rear section of the structure resembled a burnt-out shell whose insides had all been painstakingly scraped away.

With a shake of her head, Cara had marched into the manager's office. It was too late to go hunting for another motel somewhere down the road. For now, this was going to have to do.

Things only became more complicated.

When she requested separate rooms for the night, the clerk shook his head.

Keeping one eye on a television show about aliens turning up in a small, desolate, southwestern town, he told them, "Sorry folks. We had ourselves a little fire here last month. Gutted almost half our rooms. This is all we got left." He gestured at the rack on the wall behind him. There was only one key dangling there. "This is our busy season," he added with pride.

Cara looked at the clerk's balding spot as he glanced back at the television set on his desk and tried to imagine how slow the rest of the year must be if a seven room occupancy represented the "busy season." A seven-room occupancy in what was now, unfortunately for her, an eight-room motel.

Standing at her elbow, Max made no secret that the situation amused him. That, and her ill-concealed discomfort over it.

"You could sleep in the car," he suggested.

It wasn't what she wanted to hear. She glared at him. "Or you could."

But Max shook his head. He pressed a hand to the small of his spine. "Bad back. My roughing-it days are over."

It was a lie, but a small one and he figured he could be forgiven. Besides, spending the night in the car was guaranteed to give him a bad back.

Yeah, Cara would just bet they were. The man was as physically fit as any she'd ever seen. Maybe even more so. There was no doubt in her mind that when he had a willing partner, consideration for his back was the last thing on the man's mind. He looked capable of making love twisted up like a pretzel.

"You try anything and you'll find out just how 'rough' rough can be," she warned under her breath, then turning toward the clerk, she exhaled in frustration. "All right, we'll take it."

His attention momentarily diverted from the flickering screen, the clerk turned the registration book around for her benefit.

"Wonderful. Sign here." He shifted slightly at the surprised look on her face. "I've been meaning to save up for a computer, but this kind of gives it the homey touch, don't you think?"

"Homey," Cara murmured. If home was some backwater, shanty town struggling its way into the second half of the twentieth century. Cara skimmed down the column of names that appeared on the discolored pages. "Looks like you've got a lot of people named Smith and Jones coming through here."

"Yup." He seemed utterly clueless about her inference. "Popular names," the clerk agreed guilelessly.

Hell, she decided, would be being stuck in a place like this for all eternity. Cara quickly signed her name, then handed the pen to Max.

He added his on the line below.

The clerk turned the register around after Max signed in and read their names.

"Welcome, Ms. Rivers, Mr. Ryker. I'm sure you'll find your stay in La Casa Del Sol a pleasant one." The way he pronounced the motel's name testified to the fact that English was by far his first and only language. He leaned over the counter to glance down at the floor.

"No luggage?" His thin lips curved in a knowing smile as he straightened up again.

"We plan to make mad, passionate love and wear

each other," Cara told him matter-of-factly. "Can we have the key, please?"

His eyes big as saucers, he mumbled, "Sure thing."

Taking the key from the battered rack behind him, the clerk held it out to Cara. But as she reached for it, Max intervened, taking the key from the clerk.

She turned on her heel and walked out of the tiny, airless office.

"What made you say something like that to him?" Max wanted to know.

She shrugged. "I thought he needed a little spice in his life."

No two ways about it, the woman definitely was not easy to read. One moment she was flippant, teasing, the next minute she was reserved, private, like a nun in training.

"I don't know what to make of you."

"Don't worry about it. We won't be together long enough for you to have to 'make' anything of me. All you need to know is that I always get my man. *Always.* Oh, and by the way, you take the sofa," Cara informed him.

"I told you," Max reminded her innocently, "I have a bad back."

She shot him a look that was clearly nothing short of lethal. "Mister, you don't know what bad is."

He laughed softly under his breath, leading the way to Room 6. "I've traveled with you for a few hours. Trust me, I know."

"All right." She blew out a breath. "I'll take the sofa."

But then they entered the small room that overlooked the highway and discovered that decorating hadn't been the management's top priority. It hadn't even made the top five list.

A huge bed dominated the room, its frayed leopard comforter clearly intended for the next size down. At the wall beside the tiny bathroom was a dresser that had seen better decades. Two nightstands that someone had obviously put together out of a box somewhere in the early seventies buffered the bed. They did not match the scarred, dark bureau.

Two lamps, one tall, one short, were perched on top, providing the illumination, such as it was.

"No sofa," she muttered. Why didn't that surprise her? Cara looked down at the floor. "I guess I should consider myself lucky that they sprang for a rug."

"That all depends on your definition of luck," Max commented.

The rug was matted down from years of wear and from all appearances, had never been cleaned. It was hard determining just exactly what color it had originally been. Currently it was mud-brown.

"The bed's big," Max pointed out. "Plenty of room for two people who don't want to have anything to do with one another to sleep on."

His phrasing caught her attention and not in a favorable way. "You don't want to have anything to do with me?"

"Just following your lead," he told her innocently.

It was just as he'd suspected earlier. Beneath the bravado and tough talk, she was more sensitive than she would have liked.

"I'm dog tired and really don't want to argue about anything anymore, including sleeping arrangements,"

he told her, curtailing, he hoped, any further debate
about who went where.

Protesting that he'd always been nothing less than
a gentleman would have undoubtedly fallen on deaf
ears anyway. He was sure that she had her own pre-
conceived notions that had little or nothing to do with
him.

"Do you want to use the bathroom first?" he offered gallantly.

She wanted a few minutes to unwind first. Away
from him. "No, you can check out if they have hot
and cold running insects coming out of their faucets."

"Glad I can do something for you."

Cara watched as Max walked into the minuscule
bathroom and shut the door. It took a little jiggling
before the lock finally caught. Two minutes later, she
heard the shower water running.

She released the breath she suddenly realized she
was holding. Sitting down on the bed, she found her
thoughts fixing themselves on what was going on behind the door. It was hard not to imagine him naked,
the water cascading down a wall of what appeared to
be solid muscle and was otherwise seen as his chest.

What the hell was the matter with her?

She needed a man, she decided. The sooner the
better. It had been a long time since she'd talked to
someone of the male persuasion in any other capacity
than something having to do with her work.

*All work and no play, Cara…*she upbraided herself.

A ringing noise broke into her thoughts. The sound
was coming from the other end of the room, and not
from the old-fashioned dial telephone that was resting

precariously on the edge of the nightstand, vying for space with the smaller of the two lamps.

The sound was coming from the jacket Max had haphazardly thrown on the edge of the bureau.

Crossing to it, she dug into a pocket and located his cell phone on the first try.

She flipped it open and placed it against her ear, not certain just why she felt it necessary to play the part of Ryker's secretary.

"Hello?"

There was silence for a beat, and then the sound of a deep, crisp masculine voice on the other end. "Hello, who is this?"

The voice had a commanding tone to it and Cara heard herself saying, "Cara Rivers."

"Oh, I am sorry, I must have gotten the wrong number—"

Cara snapped to attention before the man hung up. "Wait, are you trying to reach Max Ryker?"

"No—" The voice paused. "Yes, yes I am. Then this *is* his cell phone?"

"Yes, it is. He's in the shower right now. Can I take a message?" She looked around for a piece of paper and a pen, then crossed to the bed and pulled her purse over.

"The shower?" Was that a chuckle she heard? "Please forgive me, I didn't mean to interrupt. I will call back later."

"You're not interrupting anything," she protested. "It's not what you think—"

She was talking to dead air. Frowning, she closed the cell phone and placed it back in Max's pocket. About to put the jacket down where she'd found it, she hesitated, wrestling with a conscience that wasn't always as vigilant as it might have been.

Self-preservation got the better of her and she began to systematically go through the other pockets in his jacket.

"Looking for something? Maybe I can help."

Startled, she nearly dropped the jacket. Intent on finding something before he was finished in the bathroom, she hadn't heard him come out.

Composing herself, Cara turned around.

And immediately became uncomposed again.

He was standing in the doorway, an almost threadbare towel draped around his hips, dipping lower where he'd tucked it in. There was still water beading on the downy hair that ran along his chest. A single ribbon of fine hair fed down his abdomen, disappearing under the rim of the towel.

The man had a stomach you could bounce quarters off of. She caught herself wondering if the same could be said of his butt before she managed to regain control of her runaway thoughts.

Cara casually dropped the jacket back where she'd picked it up. "Your phone was ringing."

And she had answered it. His eyes darkened just a shade.

"Who was it?"

She shrugged, looking straight at him, knowing that if she attempted to avoid looking his way, Ryker would find it amusing.

"He didn't say. I told him you were in the shower and he apologized for interrupting. I guess he thought you were entertaining."

Rather than say anything, Max crossed to where

she'd dropped his jacket and took his cell phone out. Flipping it open, he pressed a button. The word Private appeared in the small LCD. That could be a lot of people, but his mind gravitated to one.

"What did he sound like?"

When was the man going to put some clothes on? And why was the room getting so damn warm? Couldn't the management at least put in some fans?

"Nice voice. Deep, cultured. Like he'd never met a dangling modifier in his life."

She was describing the king. It had been more than a week since he'd gotten the assignment and he hadn't checked in with his uncle because he'd wanted something positive to report. Not that he was on Weber's trail, but that he'd captured him.

Max supposed that he should have called. It wasn't fair to leave the king twisting in the wind, although as far as patience went, his uncle seemed to possess an infinite supply. The man had gone through a great deal in the last year, the worst of which was facing the loss of his beloved only son and heir, although King Marcus still hadn't given up hope that Lucas was alive. The plane Lucas had been flying had gone down in the Colorado Rockies and so far, only bits and pieces had been recovered.

The king believed that no news was good news, even though he prayed nightly for word. The last he'd heard, his uncle was still praying.

Colorado.

He glanced toward Cara.

The man was having an unnerving effect on her, standing around half naked like that and staring at her. Cara looked at him with all the coolness she could muster. Given the situation, she thought she did rather well.

"Are you planning on dripping dry, or do you intend to get dressed sometime in the next decade or so?"

He raised a dark, inquisitive brow, throwing her into a tailspin.

"Does this make you uncomfortable?"

She shrugged, refusing to give him any satisfaction, even if something in the pit of her stomach was turning cartwheels.

"Not particularly. If you want to walk around in your birthday suit, that's up to you. I just want to go on record as saying that I sleep with my gun under my pillow and I tend to be rather jumpy where there're any sudden moves involved." She purposely dipped her line of vision to take in the towel he had draped around his hips and parts beyond.

"I'll keep that in mind." Turning around, he reached for the clothes he'd hung on the hook behind the bathroom door and took them down. "It's all yours. No insects." He walked past her, then added in a stage whisper, "Just one small mouse."

"The only rodents that make me uneasy are rats." Her eyes locked with his. "Big ones."

His laugh followed her into the bathroom, skimming along her skin even after she shut the door and took her clothes off.

Perhaps more so.

Cara took a quick shower, washing the dust of the road from her body as fast as she could. She was toweling herself dry in less than five minutes. Rather than securing the towel around her the way he had, she hurried back into her clothes if for no other reason than she could swear she could smell him on the now-damp towel.

It made her uneasy, wrapping the towel around herself.

Dressed, her hair damp and curling around her face, she opened the door. Nine minutes, start to finish, she silently congratulated herself.

Max had his back to her and was talking in a low voice. It took her a second to realize he was on his cell phone. So he'd known who was calling. Probably his mysterious client, the one who wanted Weber taken back to Monticello, Montebello, or wherever it was he'd said he was taking the man.

Over her dead body, she countered pugnaciously. Weber was going back to Shady Rock, Colorado, and that was that. The ten thousand dollars she was going to get was earmarked for Bridgette Applegate and Cara meant to get it to her or die trying. She owed Bridgette a lot.

Bridgette Applegate was the last woman who had taken her in. Unlike the others, Bridgette hadn't been part of the foster care merry-go-round. Bridgette had been a woman she'd met while she'd lived under that bridge in Denver, fighting off a fever of 103. Broke, desperate, she'd tried to take Bridgette's purse and had collapsed in the struggle when Bridgette had fought back. She was close to being unconscious.

Rather than call the police, Bridgette, a part-time nurse, had taken her home, put Cara in her own bed and tended to her as if she was her own daughter instead of a would-be mugger.

After she got well, Bridgette insisted she remain

with her until she figured out just what it was she was going to do with her life now that she was no longer going to throw it away. Bridgette Applegate had been the turning point in her life, the reason she believed in good instead of caving in before evil.

And now Bridgette needed her help and she was damned if she wasn't going to come through for the woman. And no sexy, flat-stomached, ripped P.I. was going to get in her way, with or without his towel.

Max sensed Cara standing behind him. As politely as he could, he ended the conversation with his uncle. Everything that needed to be said had been covered, in terse, veiled language, leaving anyone eavesdropping in the palace and beyond in the dark.

True, he still didn't know why he was bringing Weber in, but all would be made clear once he was on Montebellan soil again. His uncle had promised as much and although Max had no desire to return to the country where the bad memories outweighed the good and his mother had been so unhappy, he knew his duty.

Besides which, he had to admit that his curiosity about the matter was getting the better of him. He considered curiosity both his failing and his talent. Without it, he wouldn't have pursued the career he had, wouldn't have been as good at it as he was.

But it also had a tendency to get him entangled in matters another man might have easily been able to walk away from.

Like letting his imagination wander and get the better of him when it came to his new roommate.

"Eavesdropping?" Max flipped his cell phone closed before turning around.

Cara strode into the room as if she owned it. She'd learned a long time ago that bravado made people sit up and take notice and think twice before attempting to run right over you.

"In case you haven't noticed, it's a small room. I don't have anywhere to go and the bathroom was becoming claustrophobic."

He liked the way her wet hair framed her face. It occurred to him that the woman was completely unaware of her looks and totally unpretentious. He'd known so many women who were, if not vain about the gift genes and nature had bestowed on them, at least always fussing with their hair, their makeup, their clothes, paying far more attention to themselves than anyone else was.

He'd yet to see Cara even glance at a mirror to check her appearance.

He smiled at her. "You mean *you* were."

Her days of being shoved into a closet had created not only an underlying fear of the dark, but of tiny, confining places as well. But she'd be damned if she was going to say anything about it to him.

Instead her eyes narrowed as she looked at his face. "You like correcting me all the time? Or am I getting some kind of a free demonstration of the way you ran that charm school of yours?"

"Neither." He rose to his feet, refusing to rise to her bait. His eyes skimmed over her. Her shirt was clinging to her chest, a damp spot where she'd failed to dry herself off forming just above where he imagined her cleavage to be. "You're dressed."

There was only one large bath towel available beside the two hand towels. Had he expected her to come out wearing the towel like a sarong? Just because he liked to flaunt his attributes didn't mean she did.

"Sorry to disappoint you, but I don't wear hand-me-downs anymore." She nodded toward the bathroom. "That includes someone else's towel."

"Anymore? You come from a large family?"

Damn, it was as if he had some kind of homing device, zeroing in on the one word she'd slipped up on.

"I don't come from any family at all, if it's any business of yours, Ryker," she informed him icily, calling an end to the conversation.

His broad shoulders rose in a blameless half shrug. "Just making friendly conversation."

The hell he was. She raised her chin. She knew exactly where he was coming from. "Prying is never friendly."

Well, maybe he was, but any information he really wanted, he could always get from his grandfather and another wild ride on the information highway. He had the urge to drape his arm around her small, ramrod straight shoulders, but he squelched it.

"Look, Rivers, you and I are going to be together for at least a little while, don't you think we should have a truce?"

Anything to get him to lower his guard again. "Fine with me."

He glanced over her head at the headboard. There were tacky posts on either side. Not aesthetically pleasing, but it might be strong enough to do the trick—if necessary.

"And in the spirit of that truce, am I going to have

to handcuff you to the bed, or can I have your word that you won't suddenly try to take off with my car in the middle of the night?''

''You have my word.'' She had no intention of trying. She intended to succeed.

After his conversation with his nephew, King Marcus replaced the telephone receiver in its cradle. He refused to believe that Lucas was dead, despite all the facts to the contrary. His son had been too full of life, too bright to have been extinguished so suddenly without a trace the way it appeared to all the world that he had.

The plane had gone down somewhere in the Rockies, but someplace, somehow, Lucas was alive. Marcus knew it in his heart. And this man, this vermin who now called himself Kevin Weber, might hold the key to that as well as many other things.

Marcus knew he would rest easier once Weber was brought back to Montebello. And Max was just the man to do it.

Chapter 6

Max liked staying abreast of current events and watched the nightly news whenever he could. But the reception on the small television set within the run-down motel room left a great deal to be desired. Mainly a picture and clear sound. Giving up, he shut the set off and decided to turn in.

He noted that Rivers seemed to be of like mind. She was already in bed. Or rather, on top of it. She looked exhausted and more than a little disgruntled. She was also still wearing the clothes she'd put on again after her shower.

He looked down at her from the foot of the bed. "Aren't you going to change?"

The mattress beneath Cara felt as if it predated the Second World War. She sincerely doubted it had a comfortable place to offer up. Turning, she laid flat on her back and laced her hands beneath her head.

Looking up, she didn't particularly like the way he was looming over her.

"I like me just the way I am."

She was playing with words again, he thought. "I meant your clothes."

Her expression remained unchanged. "I like those just the way they are, too."

He wondered if she enjoyed being perverse and decided that she must. She was so good at it. "What do you normally sleep in?"

"A bed."

Games, she was in the mood for games. Crossing to his side of the bed, Max dipped into his dwindling supply of patience and tried again. "What do you have on when you get into bed when you're home?"

"Generally a very tired expression."

And then it hit him, she wasn't playing games, she was being evasive. And he had a feeling he knew why. "You sleep in the raw?"

Cara felt freer that way, but it wasn't any business of his that she did. She knew she should just turn her back on him and ignore the question, but something goaded her to respond.

"What of it?"

He gave her a careless shrug. "Just a coincidence, that's all. I sleep in the raw, too." Sitting down on the bed, he took off his socks and then began unbuttoning his shirt.

An edgy feeling caught hold of her stomach. Cara propped herself up on her elbow. "Well, not tonight you don't, Ryker. Stop right there," she ordered him.

He'd already peeled off his shirt and was sitting there, bare-chested. She forced her eyes to his face.

"What are you afraid of?"

"Nothing," she snapped. "Because you're not going to do anything." It was an order, not an observation. "Except to lay down on your side and drop off to sleep—now."

The dulcet tones were certainly missing. He laughed. "You're going to make one hell of a mother someday, you know that?"

She took offense at his tone. It was her heart's longing to have children. And to give them all the love she'd never had, the love she'd been storing up all these years.

"Yeah, I will. And let me worry about that, you just get some shut-eye. Now. Or I'll leave without you." The threat slipped out before she could think to stop it. She didn't ordinarily overplay her hand. She told herself it was because she was tired.

"You can't. I have the only set of keys."

Max held them up for her benefit. Then, he made an elaborate show of pushing them down deep into his front pocket. He knew she wouldn't attempt to go digging there while he was asleep.

She looked at where he'd tucked the keys. Her mouth curved wryly. She knew exactly what he was thinking. "Aren't you afraid of sustaining permanent injury if you should roll over during the night?"

He laid down on the bed. "I'll risk it."

Cara was acutely conscious of the way the mattress had dipped down, acutely conscious of the man laying less than two feet away from her.

"Does that mean you don't trust me?" she asked flippantly.

His eyes met hers. "No more than you trust me."

Something tightened within her. She inclined her head. "Fair enough."

Lying back down, she realized that he'd propped himself up on his side and was looking at her. A jittery feeling snaked its way through her body. And then Max moved closer to her until the top of his torso was almost directly over her. Her heart began to hammer harder than she was happy about, the beat keeping abreast of the throbbing in her pulse.

She needed him back in his space, not invading hers. "Unless you're looking to pick bullets out of your teeth, Ryker, I'd back off right now if I were you."

Max heard the slight thread of tension in her voice, felt the crackle of electricity between them. "You need to relax, Rivers."

The jerk was being condescending, as if he could read what was in her mind. How could he? *She* couldn't even read what was in her mind right now. Except that she didn't want him so close to her. "And you need to back off, Ryker. Now."

He didn't move a single muscle. "Is that a challenge?"

Was she going to have to fight him off after all? Every muscle in her body tensed. "If that's what it takes to get you back on your side."

She had pretty eyes, Max thought. Even when they darkened. He'd never been partial to blue-gray before. "You know, as a young boy, I could never resist a challenge. My mother said I was a constant source of worry for her."

His mother used to despair, he remembered fondly, that he would die an early death, led there by his own recklessness. Instead she had been the one to die too early, through no fault of her own.

"At least you had a mother," Cara heard herself murmuring, her voice hardly audible above the rushing noise in her ears.

She knew she should push him away, knew that all it would really take would be one quick turn and a well-placed flexing of her knee and any impromptu moves on his part would be summarily terminated.

But curiosity got the better of her. Curiosity and a strange physical pull that crept out of nowhere and presented itself to her with his name on it. Desire unfolded within her like a deck of cards being fanned out before a magic trick took place.

"You have a death wish." Her lips practically touched his as she uttered the declaration.

"Maybe."

And maybe he just had an insatiable thirst to discover what it felt like to kiss her. An insatiable thirst that wouldn't be quenched until he found out on his own what her lips tasted like.

And then he wasn't speaking any longer and neither was she.

Contact occurred and the air around them suddenly became even warmer than it already was, its edges singeing the instant their lips met.

He gathered her to him. Or perhaps she pulled him in toward her. The logistics weren't clear. They overlapped. All that mattered was that they occurred.

He tasted of something dark and sweet and compelling. She felt like she was a dried flower getting its first taste of summer rain with the promise of more lingering in the air.

Cara wound her arms around his neck, telling herself she was anchored in reality so it was all right if, just for the moment, she lost herself in this sensation. Purely for reasons of edification. A woman always had to know exactly what she was up against.

Max felt Cara's heart hammering against his chest as he drew her still closer against him, felt the heat of her body infiltrate his.

Or maybe that was his heart suddenly going into double-time. He couldn't tell. He'd done this simply on a whim, because he couldn't resist certain challenges, just as he'd told her. But once he'd thrown his hat in the ring, he found himself being sucked in completely as he reached to retrieve it.

If he'd had socks on, she would have knocked them off. Or at least curled them.

What he was entirely certain of was that Cara Rivers had created this itch, an itch so intense, it was almost impossible to scratch.

Or to bury.

But he knew he had to. Business and this kind of thing really didn't mix.

More's the pity.

Okay, time was up. It was time to come up for air, Cara's brain pleaded, before it became completely oxygen deficient.

With more than a little effort, Cara finally managed to wedge her hands against his chest. She pushed with all her might, which, to her surprise, had decreased considerably. Still, she did manage to create a very small space between them.

She could only pray she didn't sound as breathless as she felt. "Curiosity satisfied?"

She certainly didn't pull any punches, Max thought. A smile curved his mouth. He ran the back of his knuckles slowly along the silky skin of her face and watched her eyes widen before she got better control over herself.

"Not in the least. Whetted, actually."

"Too bad," Cara said, finding a ribbon of strength to tap into. She pushed him back even farther, then struggled up into a sitting position. "Because that's all she wrote."

Intrigued, Max drew his thumb along her bottom lip, allowing his mind to wander a little further. Watching her veiled reaction in her eyes. There was a complete untapped vein of sensuality right before him.

"I don't think so."

"I'm not interested in what you think, Ryker. Just in what you do. And for your own well-being, what you should do is go lie down on your side of the bed." She felt under her pillow and produced her gun. She pointed it at him, leaving the safety on. "Now."

He didn't believe in forcing himself on someone. Especially someone with gun, safety or no safety. Besides, the world seemed to be just the slightest bit tilted at the moment. Just like in the bar last night. Except that this time, he hadn't been deliberately drugged by anything. Only her.

He struggled not to show Cara that he was searching for his bearings and that she was the cause of this disorientation.

"I never argue with a lady."

"Hah," was her only response. What a crock. He'd

argued with her the better part of the time they'd been together.

With exaggerated movements, she turned her back on him and punched up her pillow. She knew damn well that she wasn't going to get any sleep tonight. But that was all right. Not sleeping fit in with her plans.

Several minutes went by. Max found that his curiosity hadn't abated. "What did you mean by that?"

She sighed. It was obvious that the man wasn't going to just peacefully drop off to sleep. He was going to give her trouble.

So what else was new?

She kept her back to him, feeling it was a lot safer that way. "Mean by what?"

"That at least I had a mother."

He would have picked up on that, she thought in annoyance. Why had she let that slip? "I wasn't speaking in tongues."

There was something defensive in her voice. His curiosity peaked, he turned around, only to find himself looking at her back. He squelched the impulse to turn her toward him. No use borrowing trouble. "Didn't you have a mother?"

She didn't bother suppressing a sigh. The man was making things difficult for her on a whole host of levels. She tried to ignore the restlessness she felt, the kind she couldn't put a name to but bothered her nonetheless. "Are you getting paid extra to annoy me?"

"I'm not getting paid to do anything at all with you," he told her mildly. "For the record, I was just being curious."

"Well, don't be."

Struggling with her exasperation, and the nameless feeling that insisted on continuing to grow within her, a feeling that might have been labeled attraction if she wasn't so damn sure it wasn't, she punched her pillow again, trying to add dimension to it. It couldn't have been flatter than if it had been run over by every single one of the wheels on an eighteen-wheeler. It was obvious that comfort was not the byword of this motel. Several attempts later, she bunched the pillow beneath her head, folding it as much as possible.

Cara stared at the rusted handle on the bureau. "No, I didn't," she finally said quietly.

He'd thought she'd lapsed into total silence. Hearing her answer, he turned back to look at her again. "Divorced?" he guessed.

She'd never known her mother or her father. She'd overheard one of the social workers say that she'd been found on a park bench when she was only several days old. Her parents hadn't even thought enough of her to leave her on a hospital or church doorstep. For all they knew, a stray, hungry animal could have come across her and ended her life before it ever began.

Cara's laugh was short and without any accompanying humor. "From me, maybe."

She could feel him propping himself up on his elbow by the movement of the mattress. There were going to be more questions. As she had done most of her life, going from one school system to another more times than she wanted to ever remember, Cara headed him off at the pass. It was always easier fighting on her own terms than waiting for the first jab to be thrown.

Refusing to turn around, to see pity in his eyes, she addressed the dingy mirror over the bureau.

"You're sharing your bed, so to speak, with a bona fide orphan. I spent the first seventeen and a half years of my life in foster homes. Sad music accompanying credits. End of story. Now go to sleep."

Her answer only raised another question. "Aren't you supposed to be in the system until you're eighteen years old?"

She could feel the hairs on the back of her neck rising. He was prying. Served her right for saying anything at all.

"Yeah."

"But you only stayed seventeen and a half—" He left the sentence open-ended, waiting for her to fill in the blank.

Annoyed, she finally turned around to look at him. Ryker seemed much too close for either their own goods. She pretended not to notice.

"I ran away for the last six months. When I was eighteen, the system was through with me." And so would life have been, if it hadn't been for Bridgette Applegate. Cara believed that from the bottom of her soul. "Now shut up and let me get some sleep before I really do shoot you."

He'd opened up old wounds. It didn't take a brain surgeon to realize that. Part of him wanted to ask why she'd run away, but he knew how dear privacy was, how precious it was especially when you were denied it. He'd been there. Had seen its effects on his mother when the press wanted to know how she felt about her husband's flagrant indiscretions.

It was in his mother's memory that he backed off. If Rivers wanted him to know the reason she ran away, she'd tell him on her own. If not, well there were a lot of questions in life that went unanswered. Such as why someone as good and kind as his mother had remained with the likes of his father. And why his father had felt the need to indulge in cheap affairs when there was someone waiting for him at home who could love him unconditionally. Someone, according to what his aunt Gwendolyn, the queen, had once told him that the duke had loved in return. But he just couldn't conquer the lust that governed him.

Since both his parents were now gone, "why" was a puzzle he wasn't destined to ever solve. And one, heaven willing, he wouldn't be destined to repeat in his own life. For apples did not fall far from their trees and children were often doomed to repeat the sins of the fathers. He knew that he would rather remain unmarried all of his life than to bring the kind of grief to a woman that he had seen in his own mother's eyes.

Max laid down again, staring at the ceiling. "Good night, Rivers."

"Good night, Ryker," she growled into her pillow.

For some reason, her response made him smile. Max closed his eyes. They had to get an early start in the morning if they were going to catch up to Weber. Lying here, wondering about the woman beside him wasn't going to help him do that.

He thought about her anyway. Eventually he managed to drift off to sleep.

* * *

The early-morning sun was just beginning to feed its way through the spaces in the curtains where the weave had thinned when Max opened his eyes again.

It felt as if he'd just closed them and he gradually became aware of his body. It ached as if he'd spent the night sleeping on a pile of stones. He supposed that getting up was actually a relief.

Stretching, Max sat up and scrubbed his hands over his face in an attempt to get his mind focused and into gear.

It was then that he realized the place beside him was empty.

Instantly alert, he looked to the bathroom. The door was closed. She was probably just in there, he told himself, but still, he was taking no chances. He knew better when it came to Rivers.

On his feet, he crossed to the paint-scarred door and rapped on it.

"Rivers, you in there?"

There was no response.

He put his ear to the door and heard nothing. No running water, no movement of any sort. An uneasy feeling got more than a toehold on him.

"Rivers?" he called again, more urgently this time. When there was still no response, he tried the knob and found it locked. Was she inside and playing games just to get to him? He had no idea how her mind worked, only that she was perverse.

"Look, if you're in there, open the damn door. Now." Still nothing. "Okay, I'm coming in. If you're in there naked, that's your problem."

Throwing his shoulder against the door, he nearly took it completely off its rusted hinges.

Cara wasn't in there naked. She wasn't in there at all.

Max cursed roundly. This definitely did not look good.

Spinning on his heel, he ran outside into the courtyard to where he'd parked his car. He knew that she could have just gotten up and was out, getting breakfast at the small café they'd passed on their way here, but somehow, he didn't think his luck was particularly running that way.

He was right.

The car wasn't where he'd left it. She'd taken it. Suppressing another curse, Max immediately checked for his keys. Shoving his hand into his pocket, he found them exactly where he'd put them.

How the hell had she managed to steal the car without the keys?

This woman appeared to have more hidden talents than a con game had angles.

Max looked around, hoping that he was wrong, that he'd somehow just forgotten where he'd parked the vehicle in the dark.

But there weren't that many places to look. He hadn't forgotten where he'd parked the car. It was gone and she had taken it.

Storming into the small office, he saw the office manager dozing in a corner, his head forward, small drool marks forging a trail down his faded shirt. The picture on his small television set was rolling so that it appeared the woman's waist was on her head as she pitched a set of knives guaranteed to cut through steel and the hardest man's heart with ridiculous ease.

Fisting his hand, Max rapped on the desk hard and the man jumped up, bumping his shins against a chair as he scrambled forward. Focusing on Max, the man blinked, then sank back into his semistupor state.

"What?"

Max knew it was useless to ask, but he did anyway. "The woman who was with me last night when I checked in, did you see her leave?"

The man stared at him slack-jawed. He scratched the stubble on his face.

"You mean she's gone?"

Well that answered that. Blowing out an angry breath, calling himself several kinds of a fool for not handcuffing her to the bedpost the way instinct had told him to, Max strode out the door.

"Does this mean you'll be checking out?" the man called after him, leaning as far over his desk as he could manage. "There's a half day charge after six in the morning, you know."

Max ignored him.

Trying to think, he walked into the courtyard again. He scanned the area, looking out onto the street, hoping against hope.

Hope died a quick, harsh death.

Rivers was nowhere in sight. Somehow, she'd managed to start up his car and make good her escape. The woman had too many hidden talents.

Hurrying back to their room Max took a fast inventory of what was there. Her things, including the laptop she'd brought in with her, were gone.

Rivers had played him for a fool.

Again.

Chapter 7

*S*tupid Americans.

Toying with his bourbon and soda, Jalil Salim looked up and studied his own face in the mirror that lined the back of the hotel bar. He watched his mouth curve in a self-satisfied smirk. It had been almost too easy. He would have enjoyed more of a challenge, wanted more of an adrenaline rush than what he'd sustained.

Did they really think they were going to catch me?

The thought seemed ludicrous. Salim raised the two fingers of amber liquid in his glass to his lips and drank deeply. He closed his dark eyes for a moment, savoring the bourbon's hot, raw burn as it made its way down his throat into his stomach.

Except for the bullet that had grazed his shoulder, the Americans had proven to be unworthy adversaries. A great deal like the fools in Montebello.

Salim set the glass down, wrapping both hands around it and hunching the thin, wiry body beneath the light gray suit, as if he meant to surround his glass. Idly he looked in the mirror and watched the people in the hotel bar come and go without really taking note of them. He was too busy congratulating himself on eluding capture.

The whole thing was rather stupid on his part, he supposed. He shouldn't have tried breaking into the Chambers ranch. It was beneath him. He should have left it to someone else. The brotherhood could have sent him someone to handle that. He had enough on his mind without looking over his shoulder, trying to elude being captured again by some would-be American law enforcement dolts. If he hadn't gotten out on bail because of a technicality, he might be rotting in jail right now.

Bail, what a foolish, foolish concept. That was why his country was so superior. It didn't have such things as bail. If you were believed to be guilty, justice was swift. It did not mince around.

Lucky for him the authorities here in the United States could be easily circumvented. Here people took you at your word and believed in an honor system.

As if they were on the same plain as he, Salim sneered into his drink. Why else would they have released him, believing that he would be back when the time for trial came.

Idiots.

Jalil laughed to himself. If those poor fools only knew what his true mission here was, they would be stunned and horrified. As well they should be. He liked the idea of striking fear into people's hearts.

Fear was a way of controlling people, of wielding power. The more fear you struck, the more powerful you were.

And he belonged to a very powerful organization. He'd been sent to this country to find a way to build up the depleted coffers of the Brothers of Darkness, the terrorist group he had pledged his allegiance to when he was just a boy. The organization was his mother, his father, his god and he would gladly die for it.

But not yet.

He sighed, frustrated. He needed to be in Austin by the end of the week. His contact would be there, the man who could put him in touch with others who thought the way he did, who believed in their cause. But it was moving far too slowly for his tastes. Finding a way to rebuild resources, to make connections that would allow a way for money to begin flowing back to his organization, took too much time.

And once that was started, he would go on to an even bigger mission. Killing the son of the king of Montebello. This time, for good. According to the intelligence network, Prince Lucas had escaped the jaws of death despite the plane crash.

But not for long.

Right now, though, Salim was getting bored, restless. From where he was sitting, he could see into a booth that was to his left. A man occupying it was there with a woman who was obviously not his wife. The man was running his hand up her skirt.

Salim shifted on the stool. He needed diversion. He needed a woman.

Being on the run this way hadn't left him much

time for the simpler, necessary pleasures of life. A man needed to feel like a man once in a while and though these western women were inferior to the women in his country and far too stubborn for his tastes, with their big breasts and tempting hips, they had their uses.

A slight movement in the mirror caused him to look to his right, toward the bar's entrance. A dark-haired woman wearing a clingy white dress walked in. The wide folds of the short dress caressed her body with every step she took. She made his mouth water.

She seemed to smile right at him, though his back was to her. Their eyes met in the mirror.

A working woman, by his estimation.

He could smell them. High-class from the looks of her. A woman who knew how to work a room, who knew how to say the things a man wanted to hear. Do the things a man wanted done. Obviously a whore, but still infinitely superior to the ones he saw frequenting selected corners and streets, offering instant gratification in the time it took to pull down a zipper.

There was a time and a place for instant gratification, but not from a common slut ripe with diseases.

He liked quality, even in his whores. Salim was willing to pay if it meant that his needs would be pleasured, that the woman was clean and attractive, not used-looking or cheap.

The very word turned his stomach. He'd had enough of "cheap" hiding in those run-down motels, staying ahead of that bounty hunter who had been after him. But now the hunter was behind him, most likely gone for good. He was through running, through with the game. The next encounter, if there was to be one, would be deadly. And he intended to be the one walking away.

The stool beside him was empty. The woman in white had crossed to him, standing behind it.

"Is this seat taken?" she purred in a voice that seemed to have been dipped in honey.

He could feel his arousal beginning. This one he would have, first quickly, then slowly, until he was tired of her.

"If you sit down, it will be."

She took it as an invitation. Smiling, she sat down beside him, adjusting her skirt so that he could see her long legs, her bare, silky skin. As she turned toward him, the neckline of her dress dipped down. The firm cleavage that was exposed to his hot gaze rose and felt seductively with each breath she took.

Salim was fairly salivating.

"Would you like a drink?" he offered.

She lowered her eyes to the one on the counter. "I'll take a sip of yours," she murmured, her voice low, husky. She took the glass from his hand. Slowly she ran the tip of her fingernail along one edge of the rim. "Is this where your lips touched the glass?"

He felt his throat and his loins tightening. "Yes."

As Salim watched, the woman pressed her own lips to the spot and took a long sip. Her eyes never left his. He found that his breath caught in his throat.

The drink was a particularly strong one. He expected to see her eyes water. Instead she merely smiled as she placed the glass on the counter.

"Smooth," she whispered. The word seemed to graze his very skin.

His arousal increased. He inclined his head toward

hers. "Perhaps you would like to leave here for a little while?"

"Perhaps," the woman echoed. Her blue-gray eyes danced as they teased his. "Just what did you have in mind?"

She was being coy. It was part of the game. "I think you know."

Leaning her elbow on the bar, she rested her chin on her hand. Her eyes smiled up into his. "Why don't you tell me, anyway?"

He skimmed her bare arm with his fingers, envisioning his hands on her breasts instead. "We could go back to my room and I could appreciate you the way a woman such as you should be appreciated."

She exhaled a long, sensuous breath, as if she could read his mind, feel his touch. His excitement mounted. "Sounds good to me." Slipping from her stool, she watched him toss a couple of twenties onto the bar before he got off his stool. She nodded at the money. "Pretty free with your money. Are there any more like that?"

His smile broadened. He'd been right. A working woman. Well, he was going to make her work.

"A great many." He placed one proprietary hand on her shoulder, steering her toward the entrance. "In my hotel room."

Her smile was inviting, seductive. "Then show me your hotel room."

Slipping his hand from her shoulder, he took her arm. "That is not all I will show you."

She leaned into him, laughing, filling his space with the perfume she'd put on only half an hour ago. "I'm counting on it."

* * *

Damn it, she was here. Intent on finding his quarry, Max had almost missed her. As if a body like that could be overlooked.

What the hell did she think she was doing?

Didn't she have any idea how dangerous the man was and what could happen to her?

Obviously not, Max thought in disgust.

The woman was a myopic fool.

Making his way out of the bar again, he followed them, keeping a discrete distance behind.

As they walked out of the bar and toward the elevator, Cara planned how and when to make her move. Weber's room was both the best place and the riskiest. Best because there was no one to get in her way, no one he could use as a shield to make his getaway. And, since the room was on the sixth floor, there was only one way out for Weber. He certainly wasn't going to leap out the window and suddenly sprout wings. This time, there would be no Dumpster to catch him.

But it was the riskiest place because there would be no witnesses, no one for him to fear if he suddenly turned on her or tried to overpower her.

The operative word here was "tried."

Which was why she had her gun very strategically planted beneath the slinky white skirt of her dress. She could easily draw it out when the time came.

Cara stole a glance at the man at her side as he jabbed again for the elevator. She'd known what he looked like, had carried around his likeness to hold up in front of people and help jar their memories, but she hadn't realized just how unnerving he was in person. There was an aura around him. Though it seemed foolish, it felt as if she was in the presence of pure evil.

It wasn't often that her imagination ran away with her.

The elevator opened. She felt his hand at the small of her back, pushing her forward. They were the only two occupants.

Cara could feel her nerves jumping. As before, she'd managed to track Weber down by the activity on his charge card. When she saw that he'd checked into the Excelsior Hotel in Dallas, she'd felt as if she'd hit pay dirt. Different than the hotels he'd stayed in previously, the Excelsior catered to a whole different breed of people. The man was moving up. Her guess was that Weber had to be feeling pretty cocky about his getaway. Maybe he actually thought he'd lost them.

Pride went before a fall, she thought smugly. Which meant that she couldn't get too confident or she would be sharing his fate.

Turning toward her, he nuzzled her neck. "How do you like to do it?"

Cara was struggling not to have her skin crawl off her body. "Slowly. All night."

He ran his hands up and down her bare arms, his breathing becoming audible, heavy. "And what will this night of ecstasy cost me?"

Steady, just a little while longer, she counseled herself. For Weber's benefit, she smiled seductively. "We'll talk terms in your room," she promised.

"Why wait until we're in my room to get started?"

Grabbing her roughly, he pulled her to him, his hand going up her skirt.

Quickly Cara pulled away. When he protested, his temper flaring, she pointed to the small camera mounted in the corner.

"Security cameras," she told him. "You don't want some underpaid, pimply-faced adolescent getting his rocks off by watching us, do you?"

He grunted something completely unintelligible under his breath as he fisted his hands at his sides and glared at the camera.

The woman with him was hot and he wanted to take her now, while his loins throbbed.

"Americans," Weber jeered. "Always watching everything. A nation of voyeurs."

Thank God for small blessings, she thought. He'd almost slipped his hand over her weapon.

Once they were in his room, Cara knew she was going to have to act fast. There would be no time for slipups and what she had going for her was the element of surprise. The man was thinking so hard with his organ that he hadn't recognized her. She'd gone through a lot of trouble not to look like herself, but a real professional would have noticed the similarities between the pro he was bringing to his room and the woman who had pounded on his door a short while ago.

Lucky for her, she thought.

Now all she needed was for her luck to hang on a little longer. There were handcuffs in her purse. It might have been safer for her to have placed her weapon in there, too, but she'd wanted to feel the reassuring press of metal against her flesh and had opted to strap her gun to the inside of her leg.

Her quarry brought her to his door, unlocking it. Anticipation rushed through his veins.

"I want you to strip for me." He locked the door behind her. "Slowly."

Cara turned around, stepping back coyly out of his reach. "We still haven't talked terms."

Pulling out his wallet, he yanked out several large bills, tossing them on the floor between them. "There. Terms. Now do your part."

It was now or never, she thought. Even if she began to go through the motions to distract him further, dropping her dress would leave her wearing matching bra and panties and a gun that didn't match either.

As his eyes bored into her, Cara began to slowly hike her skirt up, swishing the material along her legs, knowing that she was going to have to be fast to get the drop on him. She hadn't gotten to where she was by underestimating the people she was up against.

Her eyes never leaving him, Cara slipped her hand beneath her skirt, her fingers securing the hilt of her gun. She froze when she heard the knock on the door. The sound vibrated in her chest, blending with the hammering of her heart.

Distracted, angry at being interrupted, Weber growled, "Yes?"

"Room service," a Southern voice twanged.

"Go away. You have the wrong room," Weber barked. "I did not order anything."

"No, sir, this is the right room," the voice insisted. "Compliments of the house. Champagne and a basket of fruit."

Weber took a step toward the woman whose obedience he'd just bought. "Leave it in the hall."

"Can't, sir. I need you to sign that you got it. Otherwise, they'll think I took it and I'll lose my job. I've got a family to support—"

"Enough!" Weber shouted. Swearing, he swung around and unlocked the door again. He looked at the table that was before the bellman. There was nothing on it. Incensed, he looked up at the tall bellman. "Where is my champagne?"

"Right here."

The next moment, the table was being shoved into Weber. Caught off guard, Weber stumbled backward and fell.

Cara's mouth dropped open in surprise. She'd been so busy not underestimating Weber that she'd wound up underestimating his pursuer.

Ryker.

It took her less than a split second to come to. Cara pulled out her weapon, training it on Weber, who was sprawled out on the floor.

"Don't move a muscle," she ordered. "Kevin Weber, you're under arrest by order of the sheriff's department of the town of Shady Rock, Colorado."

Max was shrugging out of his bellman's jacket. There was a gun in one hand and she saw the handcuffs at the back of his belt. "He's my prisoner, Rivers," he informed her as he tossed the jacket aside.

She smiled at him serenely, shaking her head. "Uh-uh. I had him first. And possession, Ryker, is still nine-tenths of the law."

On the floor, Weber looked angrily from the call girl to the bellman. "Who the hell are you people?"

Cara smiled broadly. She really enjoyed saying this line. "Your worst nightmare, Weber." Gun trained on the man on the floor, her eyes pinning him in place, she asked, "What are you doing here, Ryker?"

He didn't want her to get away with it, but right now wasn't the time to challenge her. If they started arguing, Weber or whoever he really was might get away.

"Trying to get back my car and my prisoner," Max told her.

She could afford to be magnanimous. Up to a point. "The car's downstairs. Valet parking. Just let me get my stuff out of it and you can have it back." She spared Ryker one quick glance. She knew her answer wasn't going to sit well with him. Too bad. She had no intention of giving up custody. "But the prisoner's mine."

The woman was nothing short of infuriating. "I can have you up on charges of grand theft, auto. Like the idea of doing time, Rivers?" He didn't tell her that he didn't want too much attention drawn to Weber, that if the police were called in to arrest her, things might get dicey about Weber and the matter of jurisdiction. Besides, when he really got down to it, he didn't like the idea of the woman being arrested. He admired her creativity and spirit. And he liked besting her on his own without outside help.

Her eyes darted to his face. And then she smiled. "You can," she allowed, sensing that he wasn't the type to follow the strict letter of the law, "but you won't. Like it or not, you admire resourcefulness."

Slowly, her gun still raised, she opened her purse. "Speaking of which, how'd you get here?"

"I got the desk clerk to sell me his car." It hadn't been easy. The man insisted on being paid a lot more than the vehicle had been worth, but he'd been desperate.

Thinking back, Cara vaguely recalled seeing an old, rusting jalopy parked in front of the motel office. It hadn't looked as if it could even run.

"You're kidding."

She was smirking. He didn't particularly like being the source of her amusement.

"I'm here, aren't I?" He had a question of his own for her. "Now you tell me how you managed to get my car started without my keys?"

She shrugged carelessly. That had been a lot simpler than sneaking out of the room with all her things. She'd held her breath the entire time, positive that Ryker would wake up and stop her before she managed to get out the door.

"I hot-wired it, only to discover a second set, deep in the folds of the seat cushion."

"I thought I lost those keys," Max muttered. "I even had a second set made."

"Where the hell did you learn to hot-wire cars?"

She supposed it did no harm to tell him. "During my nomadic childhood, I lived with the family of an auto mechanic. He showed me a few things that he thought might come in handy. How to tune up a car, how to jump-start it if the battery's dead—"

"How to hot-wire it if you can't steal the keys, too." The whole story sounded incredible. He had a feeling she was lying to him on principle.

"No, he thought showing me how to hot-wire a car would come in handy if I lost my keys," she corrected. Realizing she'd turned her eyes away from Weber, she looked back and saw that the man was inching his way over to a chair. She cocked the hammer of her gun, aiming it directly at his heart. "Don't even think about it. On your knees, Weber," she ordered.

Holstering his gun, Max took out his handcuffs, but Cara beat him to it and slapped her own cuffs on Weber. Slipping them on Weber's wrists, she tested their integrity before stepping back.

"I'm impressed," Max said to Cara.

She couldn't quite gauge by his tone if he was mocking her or not, but it didn't matter. "Just stay out of my way."

Max loomed over her. She might be clever, but if she thought he was backing off, she was also very naive. "Afraid I can't do that."

Her brows narrowed. "And I'm afraid you have no choice. He's my prisoner, not yours, and he's going back to Shady Rock. I need that ten thousand dollars."

She kept throwing that number around. "What ten thousand?" he wanted to know.

"The ten thousand dollars bounty that Phil Sanford is willing to pay for his safe return before the trial. Phil stands to lose a lot of money if I don't get this scum back in time." She looked at Weber. "Get on your feet," she ordered. "Now." Cursing her ancestry and her soul, Weber rose. "Like you're doing this for the fun of it," she jeered, glancing at Max.

"I'm doing it because I made a promise."

She didn't know if he was serious or not, but his reasons didn't really interest her. Only the ten thousand did. "And I'm doing it because that ten thousand dollars means an awful lot to someone I care a great deal about. To her, it's the difference between life and death."

She was pulling his leg, he thought, trying to play on his sympathies. But the look in her eyes was so sincere, he wasn't sure. What he did know was that arguing over this was wasting precious time.

"All right then, let's go."

She made no move to go. "You're not coming with me."

"The hell I'm not."

The next thing he knew, she was pointing the gun at him.

Chapter 8

"No," she said very evenly. "You're not. I'm not about to take a chance on losing him again. Weber has a date with the sheriff in Shady Rock and that's where we're going. Without you."

Though he'd raised his hands to placate her, Max was certain that Cara wouldn't pull the trigger. He'd looked down more than one gun barrel in his lifetime and was a fairly good judge when it came to the person who trained the weapon on him.

It wasn't that he thought the woman holding the gun was all talk and no action, he already had proof of the contrary. But he also felt that she wasn't a cold-blooded killer.

His eyes met hers. "You don't have a car," he pointed out calmly.

Damn it, why did he have to keep showing up and messing everything up? If not for him, she would have had Weber in her custody over two days ago.

"I have yours."

Max lowered his arms slowly, though he didn't move forward. Just in case he was wrong.

"One step away from grand theft, auto," he reminded her. "And I think you probably know that the police have no soft spot in their hearts when it comes to bounty hunters."

Her mouth curved disdainfully. "Oh, like they're completely enamored with private detectives."

He lifted one shoulder, letting it drop carelessly. Watching Weber on the floor, Max continued to keep a respectful distance from her weapon. "I don't need the police to be enamored with me. I'm not the one who stole a car."

She blew out a breath. Ryker probably hadn't had time to file a report anywhere, but that was his registration in the car. All he had to do was get on the phone and report his car stolen. She didn't have time to take an indirect route back to Shady Rock, she had a deadline to beat. If Weber wasn't in court in three days, the bondsman forfeited his bail and she lost the ten thousand.

Cara glared at him. "I can rent another one."

"That's going to take time. And you have a prisoner in tow. That doesn't exactly make a rental agency eager to do business with you. Why go through the hassle? And one more thing," he said as she began to respond. "You know if you walk out that door, I'm going to follow you. You might as well have me next to you where you can keep an eye on me than turning around and looking over your shoulder all the time."

Max looked contemptuously at the man on the

floor. If the man's real name was Weber, then he was the Easter Bunny.

"Besides, with this one, it wouldn't hurt to have two sets of eyes watching him. He looks like the kind who'll slit your throat if you let your guard down even for a minute."

Cara took a deep breath. He was right. On several counts. But she still didn't feel easy about the arrangement. And she questioned his reasons.

"Why would you do anything for me?" she wanted to know.

"Not for you," Max said honestly, "but for a fellow human being. I hate to see a life wasted." And after looking into Weber's eyes, there was no doubt in his mind that the man could kill as easily as he could breathe, with no compunction whatsoever. "Besides, maybe I can talk some sense into your sheriff and get Weber released to me—since you won't listen to reason."

"Once Weber is behind bars and I get my ten thousand, I don't care if you go dancing with the sheriff—or Weber," she added.

Cara chewed on her lower lip, debating. What Ryker said made sense she supposed. But if the tables were turned and she talked him into letting her come along, she knew she'd try to get Weber away the first moment the opportunity presented itself. It didn't matter that she was beginning to be really attracted to the guy. Another time and another place, if things were different... But they weren't. The bottom line was that, handsome or not, Max was the competition, if not the enemy. She was going to have to be on her toes.

"Okay, Ryker, you can come along. But just as long as we're clear on one fact: You try to take him from me and I will shoot you."

He lowered his eyes to her weapon, then raised them again to hers.

"I never doubted it for a second." Passing Cara, he reached over and grabbed Weber by the arm, dragging him up. The gun in his other hand was a silent warning to the man not to try anything. "On your feet, scum." Out of the corner of his eye he saw Cara cross to the phone and pick it up. "Who are you calling?"

She held up her hand for him to be quiet as she heard someone on the other end pick up.

"Front desk? Room 618 is checking out. Quickly. Just put the tab on his credit card." Hanging up, she saw the questioning look on Max's face. "I hate loose ends. Why not let them know that he wasn't going to be here? Someone else can use this room." And then she grinned. "Aren't credit cards wonderful?"

She knew that Ryker had to have tracked Weber here the same way she had, by the man's unwitting use of his credit card. Pausing to raise her skirt, she holstered her weapon, not unaware that Ryker was watching her every move and that there was an appreciative look in his eyes.

She had to admit that, in part, she was playing up to it.

Lowering her leg, she adjusted her skirt, allowing it to fall back into place. There was an amused smile on her face.

"Careful, Ryker, or your eyes are going to fall out of your head."

It was beyond him how she could move so fluidly under the circumstances. He couldn't picture moving around with a gun between his legs.

"Doesn't it chafe that way?"

The question almost made her laugh. "Let me worry about that."

To his surprise, she took out her key and unlocked one of the handcuffs on Weber's wrist.

Had she changed her mind about leaving? "What are you doing?"

As Max watched, she snapped the cuff on her own wrist. "Making sure that Weber doesn't go anywhere without me." She looked at Max innocently. "Ready? Let's go."

Before he could say anything, she passed him and went out the door, pushing Weber out before her.

They made an unsettling trio walking through the lobby, the woman in white handcuffed to the thin, well-dressed man in gray, with the tall, dark, solemn-faced man flanking him on the other side. They garnered more than their share of stares as they made their way to the front entrance.

Bypassing the revolving door, they took the regular one, going through it single file. The man in the gray suit was between them.

Once outside the entrance, Cara produced a ticket from her purse and handed it to Max.

"What's this?"

"Your car, or it will be once the valet drives it up." She shifted slightly, wishing she had on something other than a clingy dress with layers of material adhering to her. The day promised to be a scorcher and traveling on the road was going to be no picnic.

Ryker was probably the type who made you roll down your windows instead of using the air conditioning.

He looked at the ticket incredulously. "You put a stolen car in valet parking."

"Borrowed," she corrected. "I placed a borrowed car in valet parking." She smiled, as if it was a no-brainer. "Made it easier that way."

It was also safely out of the way rather than in plain sight the way it wouldn't have been if she'd parked it on one of the adjacent streets.

"Borrowed," Max repeated, shaking his head. The woman was in a class by herself. "And just when did you intend on returning the 'borrowed' car?"

Also simple. "After I brought my man in."

"Where would you know where to find me?" he pressed, wanting to see how far she would carry the charade out. He thought she was just making this up as she went along. But to his surprise, she rattled off his address. "How did you—?"

She looked at him as if he had suddenly turned simple-minded. "The registration is in the glove compartment," she reminded him. Cara pointed to the uniformed man hurrying toward them. Dressed in green livery complete with a hat, the valet looked as if he was barely out of high school. "Give the ticket to the nice man and we'll be on our way."

Coming to a halt before them, the valet seemed to immediately hone on the steel bracelet linking Cara and Salim together. His eyes grew large.

"Are those handcuffs?" he asked in almost hushed reverence.

"Magic trick gone bad," Cara told him matter-of-factly.

"We've got a hacksaw around here somewhere," the valet offered, his eyes bobbing up and down like tiny black bouncing balls from her face to her cleavage.

Because the attention the valet tendered was so awkward and fumbling, Cara found it almost sweet. She smiled at him and could have sworn that he blushed in response.

"Don't worry yourself about it. It's under control." She slanted a look toward Max. "Give him the ticket, Ryker."

"I am being taken prisoner against my will," Weber suddenly yelled, pushing himself forward.

Though Salim was handcuffed to Cara, it was Max who pushed him back with the flat of his hand.

Surprised, the valet looked from Cara, to the man she was handcuffed to, to the other man with them, clearly in a quandary.

"Help me and I shall reward you," Weber promised urgently.

Cara twisted Weber's arm behind his back while smiling sweetly at the valet.

"Don't let him fool you," she warned. "Kevin kids like this all the time. We're professional actors. We give shows in front of children's groups all over the state. Kevin just did a line from *A Thousand and One Arabian Nights*. Pretty good, wouldn't you say?"

"Yes, ma'am, um—" At a loss who to believe, the valet plucked the ticket from Max's hand and hurried off to retrieve the car that corresponded to the number on it. He was too nervous to look back.

One corner of Max's mouth curved upward. "*A Thousand and One Arabian Nights?*"

She shrugged. "It was the first thing that came to mind."

It had just popped into her head when she'd looked at Weber's olive complexion. It struck her that the man looked a little like he might have come from some country in the Far East.

She had no idea how close to the mark she'd come, Max thought. There was no doubt in his mind, now that he had seen "Weber" and listened to him speak that the man had to have originated from Tamir, the small island country that was not too far from Montebello. There were dark forces that originated from Tamir, forces that formed terrorists groups who disagreed with the current house in power there. And with nearly everyone else as well.

Silent up until this outburst, Weber cursed their souls to eternal hell.

"You will pay for this," he growled. "Both of you." He glared at Max contemptuously, his eyes becoming tiny, dark slits. "Especially you."

"No," Cara corrected. "You'll pay—or at least the bail bondsman will."

She looked from the prisoner at her side to Max, getting an uneasy feeling that there was a piece of the puzzle that she was missing or had somehow overlooked. Was she going to be in any kind of danger, going off with these two? Had she let her guard down already with the wrong person?

"You two know each other?" Weber lapsed into sullen silence. Turning, Cara looked at the private detective. "Well?"

He'd never seen Weber before he'd dispatched to bring him home. But that wasn't to say that Weber didn't know him. Half of Europe probably did, thanks to the tabloids. It had made big news when he'd disappeared off the face of the earth, only to eventually turn up in the States. "By reputation."

Cagey, she thought. He wasn't really answering her. "So what's he supposed to have done?"

He might have not known "Weber" but he knew his type. "Blown up a few things," Max said matter-of-factly.

She looked at Weber just as the valet finally drove up Max's car.

"Are you a terrorist, Weber?" There was a momentary flash of recognition in his eyes, but only surly silence met her question.

The valet hopped out of the black sports cars, looking at it enviously. He held the keys out to Max.

"It's all yours." He grinned from ear to ear like a friendly puppy when Max took the keys from him and handed him a twenty-dollar bill. "Sure I can't get that hacksaw for you?"

"We're sure," Max told him. He realized that Cara was moving toward the driver's side. "Where do you think you're going?"

She stopped, her hand on the driver's door. "I'm driving."

"Not attached to him you're not. Besides, it's my car, remember?" He could see that she was debating unhandcuffing herself so that she could take control of the vehicle. But her desire not to lose control of the prisoner won out.

"I'll get in the back," she muttered.

Max nodded. "Good idea."

She pushed Weber ahead of her into the vehicle,

then slid in after him. It was going to be a long trip, she thought.

She shouldn't have had the extra large cola.

Her thirst had been overwhelming and gotten the better of her. When they had pulled into the last drive-through, over two hours ago, she hadn't really cared about getting anything to eat, but she had been eager to get something to drink.

Now she regretted it.

She needed to go to the bathroom. Bad. But there was no way she was going to bring Weber into the rest room with her. Neither did she want to leave him outside with Ryker and take a chance on being left stranded at some rundown gas station on highway 25, halfway between Colorado and hell.

Cara squirmed as discreetly as possible, telling herself it was merely a case of mind over matter. If she could just wrap her mind around something else, this urgent feeling she had wouldn't matter.

They'd driven in relative silence for the last hundred miles, rock songs from the eighties on the radio filling the emptiness within the car. The emptiness outside the car was almost overpowering.

In the distance, to the far left, Max saw what looked to be a vulture circling over something. It didn't give him a warm feeling.

This truly was a desolate country, he thought. At least, large sections of it were. His own country was little more than the size of New Mexico itself, with about as many people. It filled him with awe to be within a country that was so large, it could fit scores of countries within its borders.

Max looked in his rearview mirror, not at the road he'd just passed, but at the woman in the back. Unaware of his scrutiny, she appeared to be in a great deal of discomfort. He smiled to himself. It undoubtedly had to do with that huge container of soda she'd consumed.

He was beginning to know the way she thought. She was probably afraid that if she took off her handcuff and made a stop at a rest room, he'd take off with the prisoner. The way, he had no doubt, that she would—unless he actually got her to give him her word. The fact that she had called room service before they left with the prisoner had shown him that she was honorable in her own way. It just took a bit of doing to tap into that honor.

As he'd told her earlier, he really wasn't sure just what to make of her.

Max glanced at the fuel gauge on the dashboard. The needle was beginning to dip below the quarter of a tank mark. They could definitely use a refill at the next station. Looking at the GPS monitor on his dashboard for his location, he hit the sign to locate the closest gas station in the area. The answer came up almost immediately. God, but he loved technology.

"There's a gas station five miles down the road." He watched her face for a reaction as he added, "What do you say we get some gas and get out to stretch our legs? I'm getting a little punchy playing chauffeur up here."

To his surprise, she looked more distressed than relieved. That didn't make any sense.

A gas station. That meant a bathroom. Oh God, why had she thought of that?

She pressed her legs together beneath the white dress, the gun digging into her skin. Cara shifted uncomfortably. "Okay by me."

They were there almost before the conversation was finished.

Pulling the car up to the pump, Max got out first. Instead of beginning to fill the tank, he opened the rear door.

"What are you doing?" she demanded.

He took her arm and ushered her out. She was forced to pull Weber in her wake, but Max stopped her before she allowed the man to get out.

"Why don't you uncouple yourself from Weber and use the facilities?" Max suggested, lowering his voice. "Maybe change out of that dress into something a little more practical?"

Although, from where he stood, he could just as easily watch her wear that dress all the way back to Shady Rock. The perspiration had the material sticking to her breasts, reminding him just why God had gone to work so diligently on Adam's rib.

She looked at him knowingly, a frown curving her mouth.

"While you take off with Weber? I don't think so." To her surprise, Max handed her the keys he had just taken out of the ignition. "What's this?"

"Car keys. You obviously don't trust me and giving you my word doesn't seem to count, so I'm giving you the keys to the car."

Cara closed her hand over the keys, looking at him. Weber was still sitting in the car, his wrist shackled to hers.

"Why?"

"Because you look like you're about to explode and I hate to see anyone uncomfortable to that extent, even you," he added, knowing she expected it. The truth was, he wasn't feeling quite as hostile toward her as he had initially. She'd impressed him with her ability to track down Weber and her ingenuity. He couldn't dislike her. "Now for once in your life, trust someone, woman, and get in there before you embarrass yourself." He pointed toward the side door marked with the words Rest Room.

Ripe comments rose to her lips, but she didn't utter them. He was right. She was going to explode and she had no choice but to trust him.

Cara pressed her lips together. "Your word?"

He looked at her. "Would you believe it?"

She took a deep breath. "Yes."

Max inclined his head. "Then you have my word." A smile slid over his lips as he looked at the keys in her hand. "And my car keys."

She closed her hand over them. "Always nice to have a backup."

He pointed toward the small convenience store. "I'll get the key to the rest room for you while you take your handcuff off. Cuff him to the strap." He indicated the overhead extension. "He won't be able to hot-wire the car from the back."

The inference was not lost on her. Quickly she fished the keys to the handcuffs out of her purse and uncoupled herself from the prisoner.

"I am not an animal," he shouted at her, yanking hard at the strap she tethered the other cuff to. It didn't give and he cursed loudly. "When I get loose, you will pay for this, whore."

"You're not getting loose," she informed him tersely, "so you might as well save your breath with those threats."

With one eye on the interior of the car, she hurried around to the back. It was all she could do to contain herself as she popped open the trunk and took out the small valise she'd tossed in there with her change of clothes.

Max emerged from the small store just as she closed the trunk. He held out the rest-room key to her. It was mounted on a huge block of wood. She snatched the key from him so quickly, she almost whacked herself with the wood.

"Five minutes is all I need," she told Max, flying by him. "Less."

With that, she hurried into the rest room, praying that she hadn't made a mistake in trusting him. She would have felt better if she'd managed to let air out of one of the tires. By the time he would have gotten it filled again, she knew she would have been able to make it out.

She glanced over her shoulder before she shut the door.

Max waved her inside. "Go," he ordered. "We'll be right here, waiting."

Muttering a fragment of a prayer that he wasn't lying and she wasn't being incredibly naive, Cara let the door close behind her.

Chapter 9

Cara's fingers flew as she shed her dress.

The last time she'd gotten dressed this quickly, the house she was living in at the time had been on fire in the middle of the night. The clothes she'd hastily thrown over her nightgown had been the first she'd owned that hadn't been hand-me-downs cast off by someone else, bought with money she'd earned herself. There was no way she was going to allow them to be consumed by a fire.

Foolish, she knew, looking back, but at the time the clothes had represented her first real step toward independence, a badge she wore with pride, and she'd hung on to them.

This time it wasn't pride that spurred her on, but fear.

Grabbing the white dress and stiletto heels, not bothering to check anything as nonessential as her makeup and hair, Cara burst out of the rest room much the way she'd burst into it a few minutes earlier. Striding quickly, she hurried back to the gas pump, half convinced that though she'd rushed and still had the car keys clutched in her hand, Max had left with the prisoner and without her.

It took a second for the sight to register.

Max was leaning against the hood of the car, obviously finished pumping gas, obviously waiting for her.

Breathless looked appealing on her, Max thought almost against his will.

"You certainly do know how to make an entrance," he commented wryly.

She took a deep breath, hoping her voice wouldn't give her away. "You're still here."

"Why shouldn't I be? I gave you my word," he replied simply. "Unlike some, I keep my word." He looked at her pointedly. "It means something to me."

"That would be a first." He raised a quizzical eyebrow at her cynical comment. Since he'd been considerate, she elaborated. "Most of the people I know don't keep their word."

That would explain a great deal. Max straightened. "Maybe you should think about getting to know a new set of people."

"Maybe." Opening the trunk, she tossed in the white dress and heels, then closed it again. "All right, let's get going."

"Not just yet." She looked at him uncomprehendingly. "My turn," he informed her easily. "Or rather, *our* turn." He peered into the back seat at Weber.

"How about it, 'Weber'? Care to have a bonding moment and accompany me to the rest room?"

If looks could kill, Max thought, the one from their mutual prisoner would be driving the last nail into his coffin even as he stood there.

"Go to hell," Weber spat.

"Possibly," Max allowed, "but not today. And, unless you're part camel, my guess is that you have to make use of the facilities as much as either one of us." Max put his hand out to Cara. "I need the key for the handcuffs. The car won't fit in there."

For a moment, she hesitated. Suspicion reared its head. Old habits died hard.

But then she took the key out of her purse and handed it to Max. After all, she still had the car keys and the car. And there was thirty miles of nothing around them. Where could he go?

The last time there had been an abundance of nothing, she reminded herself, Ryker had managed to find transportation. A car, it had turned out, that only had enough life left within it to reach her. They'd left it where it had died. But that didn't negate the fact that the man seemed to lead a charmed life. She couldn't help but admire that. And him, though she didn't dwell on that. Extraneous emotions only got in the way.

She held her breath, watching him.

Max unlocked the handcuff that was attached to the overhead strap inside the car and snapped it around his own wrist. He tugged on the handcuff to get the prisoner moving. The latter looked at him malevolently.

"Let's go, 'Weber.' I'm not going to enjoy this any more than you are."

When they came back out again several minutes later, Max found Cara leaning against the building, situated less than five inches away from the rest room door. She made no effort to hide the fact.

He shook his head. "Still don't trust me?"

"Oh, I trust you," she assured him innocently. "I just got lonely."

Max laughed and shook his head. "Right."

Her eyes slid over to Weber. The man was becoming surlier with every mile that went by. He looked capable of killing them both where they stood. "Did he wash his hands and remember to behave?"

"He was a perfect gentleman—after a slight debate." Max strode to the car, pulling Weber in his wake, then stopped short of the driver's side. He looked back at Cara. "Tell you what. I'm beat. How about I stay in the back with our friend here and you drive? And take that suspicious look off your face, I'm not trying to put anything over on you, I'm just tired of driving, that's all."

She held up her hands in mute protest. "Never said a word."

"No, but you thought it."

He was right, she had. Cara opened up the driver's side and got in.

"So when did you become a mind reader?"

"Too general a term," he contradicted. "I'm not a mind reader. But I can read women." Opening the rear passenger door, he pushed Weber in first, then got in himself.

She would have thought as much. What kind of a woman appealed to Ryker, she wondered. Did he like leather or lace? To wrestle or to play the conqueror? It was hard to say, he gave out too many signals and not enough information.

"Do much 'reading' in your spare time?"

"Enough," he answered.

She could hear the smile in his voice. A man who looked the way he did probably had women strewn all around like dirty socks in a bachelor pad. Didn't matter to her how many dirty socks he had scattered around, she told herself. Nope, not one wit.

Turning the key in the ignition, she stepped down on the accelerator and tore out of the gas station.

Thrown back against his seat, Max caught hold of the back of the driver's headrest and leaned forward.

"Hey, Mario Andretti, we're not going to make Shady Stone—"

"Rock," she corrected tersely, her eyes glued to the darkened road.

"Whatever, before nightfall no matter how fast you drive so you might as well slow down." Damn it, he'd forgotten that the woman drove like a maniac. "Something along the lines of the speed of sound would be nice."

He was right. The man was making a habit out of it. Holding her tongue, she eased back from the gas pedal. She had no idea where that burst of uncharted energy had come from.

The nearest town with any law-enforcement officials turned out to be almost one hundred miles away. La Cuchara Del Oro. The golden spoon.

"Sounds more like a restaurant than a town," Max commented when she told him the name. He looked at the prisoner. "Maybe we can just leave him in the freezer overnight."

He was kidding, but housing the prisoner could be a problem, which was why she'd targeted the town they were going to. It was the only town on the way with a jail cell.

"I figure your people want him alive as much as mine do. That means if we want to get any sleep tonight, we need a cell to put him in."

But something else she'd said had already caught his attention. "What do you mean, my people?"

If Cara didn't know any better, she would have said he was being touchy. Probably just the monotony of the road getting to him. Even the songs on the radio had begun to repeat themselves for a third time since they'd started on this trip.

"Your client, the people or person from Monticello who sent you to bring this guy back. What else could I mean?"

"Montebello," Max corrected automatically.

When she'd said "your people," he'd thought that she'd recognized him. Maybe he was being needlessly paranoid, but he didn't want to be associated with his father's country. Though he didn't include his brother or his uncle's family, for the most part the people born to royalty had always struck him as a group of vain, empty-headed people who were in positions of power and luxury through no actual effort of their own other than being lucky enough to be born to that world.

He hadn't considered himself lucky to be born to

it. He considered himself cursed. Cursed because there was almost always a spotlight to record not just the good moments, but the bad. Especially the bad. Cursed because he hadn't been free to do what he'd wanted to do, but had always been reminded by his father to "set an example."

Right, an example, like his father had with all his flagrant marital transgressions, his endless parade of mistresses.

"Something wrong?" Cara asked, looking at his face in the rearview mirror.

His eyes met hers in the mirror, his face noncommittal enough to play winning hands of poker with. "No, why?"

She shrugged, feeling stupid to have been concerned. "No reason. You just had a funny look on your face, like you're working up your anger."

He looked at Weber, who had taken one side of the car and was now apparently sleeping. Just like that. "My anger doesn't need to be worked up, it needs to be toned down."

She took him at his word and decided that for the time being, she would leave him to his thoughts.

Sheriff Joe Adler took off his hat and scratched his balding head. A good-natured man with the body of a well-ripened pear, the request put to him by this young woman had left him baffled.

He looked from one handcuffed man to the other. "Which one's the prisoner?"

Cara laughed. "The smaller one. Then you'll hold him for me until morning?"

Joe seemed genuinely sorry to offer them any less

than complete cooperation. Finally, a decent man. Cara felt like proposing to him, but he was probably married. The best ones usually were.

"I dunno, I've gotta look this up in the rule book, ma'am. I'm kind of new at this," the man confessed. "Won the election unopposed," he told them both in a whisper. "The last man didn't want the job anymore and so now it's mine."

She knew every aspect of her job, knew just where she could rely on the law and where she was on her own. This was one small area where the police department was required to come through. That was why she had made sure she had all of Weber's paperwork in hand before she got rolling.

"Trust me," Cara said, "we can leave the prisoner here overnight. I have all the appropriate paperwork with me, signed and notarized."

As Max watched, she produced several official documents from her gargantuan purse, testifying that she was acting on behalf of Philip Stanford, a licensed Colorado bail bondsman as well as at the behest of the Shady Rock sheriff's department. She showed Adler the original bounty poster with Kevin Weber's likeness plastered all over it.

"This is his offense," she said, pointing to the paper where the official charges were drawn up. She let the sheriff look over the sheet before continuing. "You don't want this man running loose in your town, now do you?"

He handed back the documents to her. "No ma'am, I don't," he agreed, then looked at Max. "How do you figure into all this?"

"You might say her bodyguard." He ignored the

incredulous look Cara sent him. "I get to watch her back."

The sheriff glanced at the kind of view that afforded and couldn't help the grin that came to his lips. He loved his wife dearly, but a man could always look. And dream a little.

"Nice work if you can get it," he murmured.

Cara walked up to the single holding cell. The very fact that there was only one testified to the fact that any crimes in Del Oro were of the venial variety. Wrapping her hand around the bars, she gave them a tug.

"They certainly feel strong enough." She turned around and tried to appeal to the man's sense of fair play. "Sheriff, I promise we'll be gone by morning. We just need a place to put the prisoner while we get a little sleep." Both of them were tired and there was no pretending otherwise. Determined as she was to get Weber back to Shady Rock, she knew her own limits. "By the way, where's the nearest motel?"

"Ain't got one. Had one," he quickly added, not wanting them to think of Del Oro as a two-bit hick town, "but it burned down. Town counsel's trying to raise funds for a new one."

That didn't do them much good tonight. "Where do people who come through stay?" she wanted to know.

"They don't. They just go through. Keeps the town peaceful," he attested. Adler looked at them for a moment, then made a value judgment. "Tell you what. You two look like decent folks. I've got a room over my garage. It's not much, but there's a bed in it and you're welcome to it. Had Martha's nephew staying with us for a while. He used the room, but he's moved on now. I can have Martha put some clean sheets on the bed for you. Martha's my wife,'' he added belatedly.

Cara smiled. "I rather thought that."

She looked at Max, remembering the last time they'd shared a bed together. Something had come over her and she'd almost made a mistake. There was no guarantee that the same something wouldn't rise up again to trouble her. But she was too exhausted to consider sleeping in the car and too tired to go back on the road to try to find suitable accommodations tonight. The room over the garage with its single bed was going to have to do.

"That's very generous of you, Sheriff. But don't you think you should check with your wife first before you make the offer?" Max suggested politely. "Mrs. Adler might not like the idea of you bringing home strangers to spend the night."

Adler's wide belly shook beneath his drooping gun belt as he laughed.

"You obviously don't know my Martha. Woman talks to flowers just to keep in training," he told Max fondly. "She'd love to talk to real people." He reached for the telephone on his desk. "But I will call her so she can have two extra places set for dinner. Martha loves company, she purely does."

"If you're sure we're not putting you out," Cara added in her two-cents worth.

Surprised by the sensitivity he'd just displayed, she looked at Max. She didn't know any other man who would have thought of asking if the man's wife was agreeable to a suggestion that was tendered by her husband, not where his own comfort was concerned.

Ryker was in a class by himself.

Max could feel her eyes boring into him. Now what had he done? "What?"

The sheriff was busy calling his wife. Turning away, she lowered her voice.

"Just trying to figure out if you're on the level. Most men I know wouldn't have given the sheriff's wife a second thought."

Sixteen hours on the road and she still smelled good enough to arouse him. Maybe this idea of sharing a bed for the night wasn't such a good one, Max thought.

"Like I said, you need to get to know a better class of people."

Adler let the receiver drop back into its cradle. A wide grin split his round face. "It's all set. She's tickled pink."

"Um, and what about my—our," Cara amended, "prisoner?"

Adler nodded at the purse where Cara had returned the documents. "Since you've got the paperwork making this all legal and tidy, we'll just keep him here, tucked away for the night like you said."

She shook her head. "No, I mean, is there somewhere we can go to get him some dinner?"

Adler waved the question away. "Don't worry about it. Martha'll rustle up something for him, too. Great little cook, my Martha." He looked at Weber. "You're in for a treat."

In response, Weber swore at him viciously.

Taken aback, Adler looked at Max. "My, he's a mean one, isn't he?"

"That he is," Cara readily agreed.

She thought of the way that Weber had looked at her in the hotel bar, the way he almost stole her air within the elevator as he was bringing her to his room. She had no doubts that he was the kind who liked his women weak, submissive and subservient. The thought made her shudder.

"You're going to need to unlock the cuffs, unless you want to spend the night with him," the sheriff told Max. The latter held out a hand to Cara. She was quick to supply the key.

Cara watched intently as the sheriff opened the cell door and ushered the prisoner inside. Max took the handcuffs from Adler and handed them to her.

Locking the door and testing to make sure it was secure, the sheriff shook his head as he turned back to look at Cara. "A lady bounty hunter. Now don't that just beat all?"

Max grinned, placing his hand to the small of her back as he began to usher her from the room. "My sentiments exactly."

"Hadley," the sheriff addressed the lone man sitting with his feet up on the scarred desk in the back room. The deputy immediately put his feet down and stood up at attention. "We got ourselves a prisoner tonight, so don't slack off and go to steal some time with that Melinda of yours. You can make eyes at her on your own time, not mine. I'll be by later with some dinner for him."

The deputy was almost salivating as he asked, "Martha's cooking?"

Adler beamed. He always liked hearing his wife being appreciated. The woman put her heart and soul into her cooking.

''Yup.'' And then he smiled at his subordinate. ''I'll have her pack a little something extra for you, too, Hadley,'' he promised.

It was a surprisingly sweet evening.

The Adlers, Cara discovered, had been together close to forty years and looked as if they would be perfectly content to spend another forty in each other's company. Their only regret, Martha didn't mind telling them, was that they had never been able to have children of their own.

Cara found herself wishing that she had met people like the Adlers when she had been in the system. Living with people who had such genuine affection for each other would have painted a completely different picture of the world for her. There would have been depth instead of shallowness, affection instead of fear.

During the course of the meal, she watched them exchange secret glances, saw the sheriff pat his wife affectionately several times and watched Martha Adler reciprocate in kind.

Words weren't necessary, they had their own brand of communication.

Serving coffee after the best meal Cara could remember having in recent history, Mrs. Adler cozied up to her guests on the worn Herculon sofa in the family room. Cara couldn't help smiling to herself. For all the world the woman looked exactly like the image she'd had as a child of Mrs. Santa Claus.

Before she'd been stripped of her fantasies and her innocence.

"So how long have you two been together?" Martha wanted to know.

"Martha, you don't ask those kinds of questions of guests," the sheriff chided.

Her eyes were almost violet in their innocence as she looked at first her husband, then the pair she was entertaining. "But how else am I going to know things, Joe?"

Max began to answer, but Cara was quick to intercede. "Five years."

"You've been married that long?" Martha asked. To Max's continued surprise, Cara nodded. "But where's your wedding ring, dear?"

All right, let's hear this one, Max thought, leaving the floor opened to her.

Cara bit her lower lip, as if she were debating admitting the woman into this portion of her life. It gave Max pause. Rivers was a great little actress. Which meant she could use her skills on him. How was he to trust anything she told him?

"We were too poor to afford a ring," Cara finally said. "When we were married by the justice of the peace, he had to used one of the judge's cigar bands." She smiled warmly at Max. "I wore it until it ripped. Now, nothing else seems good enough to replace it."

There were tears in Martha's eyes. She placed her hand over the sheriff's. "Is that the sweetest thing you've ever heard, Joe?"

Her husband nodded in agreement.

Max shut the door behind him to the small room the Adlers had brought them to. It was a step up from

the last motel room they'd shared. Smaller, it had only
a tiny shower stall and toilet for a bathroom, but it
was bright and clean and reflected the same kind of
love he'd witnessed in the Adlers's home.

His mother would have thrived with a man like
that, he thought. She would have been far better off
if she'd fallen for someone as simple as Joe Adler
rather than losing her heart to a dashing prince who
never realized the gift he'd been given.

Turning around, Max looked at Cara. The woman
was a constant source of confusion for him. "Why
did you tell them we were married?"

She would have thought he'd understand.

"That was a sweet, conventional woman and I
didn't want to shock her. The sheriff said there was
only one bed," she reminded him. "It doesn't matter
what century it is, that woman is of the mom-
baseball-apple-pie generation."

He supposed he could see her point. But where had
the details come from? "Cigar band?" he queried.
"What made you come up with that?"

Cara laughed softly to herself. "Saw it in a movie
on TV once. At the time I thought it was hopelessly
romantic. When the couple finally got rich, he bought
her a wedding ring fashioned exactly like a cigar
band, using diamonds and rubies to form the Indian
chief's features." She remembered praying with all
her heart that there would be a man like that in her
life someday.

"You don't strike me as the type to like sentimental things like that."

When she turned around, she found he was right

behind her. There wasn't all that much space in the room. It was difficult not to bump up against each other.

Taking a step back, she tossed her head, shutting down. She had to learn to stop sharing tiny things with him. It compromised her somehow.

"I'm not." Cara indicated the bed. "Same arrangement as last time?"

He'd taken the right side, she the left. "Fine with me."

The problem was, she thought as she lay down half an hour later, that it really wasn't fine with her. The bed was smaller than the one in the motel room, the walls were closer and as for him, well, Ryker was far too close for comfort.

It didn't look as if sleep was going to be in her immediate future, Cara prophesied, scrunching up her pillow beneath her.

She was wrong.

She was asleep within ten minutes.

It was Max who couldn't sleep.

Chapter 10

"No, Ted. Don't. Please, don't. Don't."

Max had just spent the last few hours watching the woman beside him sleep, alternating between feeling something for her he didn't want to put into any sort of a context and being aroused by Cara's close proximity. Just when he thought it was hopeless, he started to drift off.

The words, the heart-wrenching plea, penetrated his brain, breaking up the haze of sleep that was beginning to descend over him.

Max woke with a start, instantly becoming aware that the woman he was sharing a bed with was thrashing from side to side as if she were desperately trying to avoid something.

Or someone.

But she was sound asleep.

Hesitating, Max thought of letting whatever she

was dreaming about play out its course. She was obviously having a nightmare and he knew that if he woke her up, Rivers would lash out at him for touching her, accusing him of trying to take advantage of her while she was asleep.

He knew without it being said that the woman was highly protective of her boundaries. If he deigned to wake her up from a nightmare, she'd probably have his head for seeing her in such a vulnerable light.

He watched her for a moment, the way he had for most of the night.

The nightmare didn't abate.

It was hard to ignore what was happening and impossible to fall back asleep when Rivers was breathing so hard. It was as if she were running.

Or suffering.

"No," she begged, her eyes squeezed shut, "leave me alone. Leave me alone." There was a barely suppressed sob in her voice.

Nightmare or not, he couldn't just allow her to agonize like this. His hand on her shoulder, Max tried to shake her lightly.

When she shrank from his touch, he tried again, a little harder this time.

"Rivers, wake up, you're having a nightmare." She moaned in response. A gut-wrenching, frightened moan. This time, he shook her more roughly. "You hear me? It's a nightmare. It's not real. Wake up."

Her eyes flew open, disoriented, huge. Terrified.

Until this moment, Max would have bet anything that the bounty hunter beside him wasn't capable of being frightened, not like any mortal woman.

But she could be.

There were tears in her eyes, he realized.

Because he was a royal and because he was his mother's son, Max had always been first and foremost a protector. Seeing the tears sliding down her cheek brought out the qualities that had been ingrained in him since childhood.

Taking her into his arms, Max held her before she was completely awake or conscious of her surroundings.

And then awareness struck. She realized she was being held. Cara immediately began to struggle, to twist and strain against him, cursing his soul to hell along with the rest of him.

"Leave me alone, Ted, or I swear I'll—"

Instinct would have him let a rattler go before it bit. But this wasn't a rattler, this was a woman, a hurting woman and Max held her tightly, talking to her as if he were trying to gentle a stray dog that had been abused. There was a soft side to his heart when it came to the downtrodden and the frightened and he refused to be pushed away.

Rivers hadn't had a nightmare, he realized, she'd had a flashback. Back to a time when someone or something had terrified her. Badly.

"*Shhh.*" He rocked with her, slowly, the way someone would comforting a child. But these were not childish fears, he knew. They were fears that belonged to a woman. "I'm not Ted. It's all right, Rivers, it's over. You're here, safe. No one's going to hurt you, you're safe," he repeated.

The sound of his voice, his words, sank in. For a moment, Cara sagged against him as relief washed over her. A dream, it had been a dream. A nightmare recreating the nightmare she'd lived through.

The one she would never be rid of, no matter how hard she tried to block it out. It found her in the night, when her defenses were down, ripping into any peace she might have found during the day.

Taking a deep breath, Cara willed herself to calm down, to steady her pulse.

And then she realized that Ryker was holding her.

Jerking back, pushing her hands against his chest to hold him in place, she looked at him accusingly. "What the hell do you think you're doing?"

Well, she was back to normal, he thought. It was like being confronted with both the lady and the tiger and he wasn't sure, in their present agitated state, which one could do the most harm.

"Trying to wake you up."

She didn't believe him. Like every other man, he was trying to take advantage of her. She should have known better than to trust him.

"Oh, right. By putting a half nelson on me?" she demanded.

He'd known this reaction was coming, but it still annoyed him. "Only way to keep you from taking a swing at me."

His answer cut through her tirade-in-the-making. "I tried to hit you?"

He laughed, shaking his head. Awake or asleep, she was definitely someone to contend with.

"Hit, bite, gouge," he elaborated. "You're hell on wheels, Rivers." And then he paused before asking, "Who's Ted?"

"Nobody," she snapped.

His curiosity was aroused. Reeled in, he didn't back off that easily. "Must have been somebody. You were pleading with him to leave you alone."

Her eyes narrowed. It was none of his business. "I said nobody. If I hit you, I'm sorry," she said tersely, then shrugged noncommittally. "Just a nightmare that got out of hand."

It was more than that and they both knew it, Max thought. His eyes never left her face. "You were crying."

Her chin went up, daring him to argue. "Probably because you were holding me too tight."

He shrugged, knowing the issue would go no further because she wouldn't allow it to.

"Yeah, probably." And then he paused, giving it one more try. "You know, if you want to talk—"

What was he, some kind of tabloid groupie trying to get a fix? "I don't."

She'd almost snapped his head off with her answer. "Right." He didn't need this aggravation. Lying down again, Max turned on his side, his back toward her. "Good night."

"Good night," she muttered.

There was no way she was going to sleep, Cara thought, frustrated. Shutting her eyes would only bring all the vivid images back. Images that had had her shaking in the night more than once.

Except that this time, she wasn't alone. She was with someone, someone who had tried, for whatever reason, to make the images go away.

She pressed her lips together, thinking. Debating.

Somewhere, she'd heard that confession was good for the soul and while she had nothing to confess in the absolute sense of the word, maybe sharing something that continued to haunt her might lessen some of its power over her.

What did she have to lose? After they got Weber back to Shady Rock, she'd never see this man again. Maybe purging a little to an almost anonymous stranger would actually do her some good.

She took a deep breath.

"Ted was my foster brother. Ted Henderson. He was the all-American golden boy, only son of the last family I stayed with."

The people she ran away from, he remembered. Max rolled over toward her, saying nothing. Not altogether sure he wasn't imagining the sound of her voice. He waited for her to say something else.

When she didn't, he prodded. "And this Ted, he's the reason you ran away?"

"Yes." Even the admission was hard for her to voice. Because if she admitted that Ted was the reason she ran away, she had to admit what he had done to her.

Max had seen the terror in her eyes before she'd focused them. He was acquainted with that look. His line of work had brought him to the lunatic fringe more than once.

"Did he hurt you?"

Did he hurt you? The question seemed to mock her. *In a thousand ways you couldn't even begin to imagine.*

Out loud, Cara admitted, "He didn't think so. He thought he was doing me a favor." Her mouth twisted bitterly. The tears came of their own accord. She wasn't even aware of them at first. "Indoctrinating me in the ways of womanhood was what he called it. I tried to fight him off, but he was too strong, too sure I was going to love it.''

Her voice caught and it took her a moment before she could continue. ''I tried to tell his mother, but she wouldn't believe me. Nobody would believe that he would do such a thing. Everybody loved him.'' The suppressed anguish gave way to anger. She swiped at the tears that refused to stop, frustrated by their advent, pained by the memory that rose in her mind. ''I was so crazy about him when I was first placed there. He was so handsome, so funny, so kind. I was so flattered when he began to pay attention to me.'' She pressed her lips together again, wrestling with the guilt. ''Maybe I didn't realize—''

''That you had done something to bring it on yourself?'' Max second-guessed her thoughts.

Cara froze, then anger flashed in her eyes. ''I didn't.''

Max wiped a tear away from her cheek with his thumb. ''No,'' he agreed softly with conviction, ''you didn't.''

But if that were true, then why had everything fallen apart so drastically for her? The Hendersons were wealthy people, they could have afforded to wait, to let nature take its course and have the baby arrive with family in attendance, she thought.

Except that no one ever knew.

''I got pregnant.'' She looked at Max defiantly, daring him to say anything derogatory. When he didn't, she continued. ''That's when I ran away. I knew they would blame me, the Hendersons. They were so crazy about their son. They would say it was all my fault for tempting him. I was afraid they were going to make me get an abortion. And I was afraid that he would try something again.'' Her voice caught as the memories came flooding back. ''So I ran away.''

''What happened to the baby?''

Her voice was small, distant. ''I lost it. I got sick and I lost it.'' She pressed her hands to her lips, trying to keep back the sobs. It had been so long since she thought of that, of the baby she never had a chance to hold, the baby she had loved from the moment she'd known of its existence—despite its origin.

There was so much love in her heart that had nowhere to go. That had never had anywhere to go.

This time, when Ryker took her into his arms, she didn't struggle, she let herself accept the comfort he offered. It was only temporary. This was only talking out loud to a man destined to disappear from her life, nothing more. She didn't have to be afraid of the consequences, didn't have to risk the hurt again.

Max held her, rocking with her, feeling for her. For the girl she had been, frightened, alone with nowhere to turn and no one to believe her.

Faced with tenderness instead of antagonism, Cara could feel herself breaking down. She began to cry. And damned herself for it as well as him. If he'd only been distant, critical, she could have kept it together.

Max sensed the internal struggle she was waging, understood the need she had to release the pain that was there.

''It's okay,'' he told her softly. ''Let it out. You can cry, no one'll know.''

''You'll know.'' Her voice was muffled against his chest.

He felt her warm breath through his shirt. The sensation made him feel closer to her. ''I don't count, Cara.''

She looked up at him, her face streaked with tears. He'd never said her first name before. The walls inside her crumbled.

''Yes,'' she said quietly, ''you do.''

Max couldn't help himself then. She'd stirred something within him, something that went beyond the boundaries of being a protector, something that spoke to him on a gut level, where he lived.

Very gently, Max brought his lips down to hers and kissed her.

He waited for her to shove him away. It was in her nature, what he had come to expect from her.

She surprised him.

Cara wound her arms around his neck and drew him to her even as she drew herself up to him, and returned the kiss with such passion, such need that it left him completely breathless.

Completely captivated.

The kiss deepened as he gathered her to him, holding her as if she were something precious, something fragile that could break at the slightest pressure. Someone he had to protect at all costs.

She could have cried, he was so gentle. And yet, there was something explosive about the way he kissed her.

A fire began in her belly, a fire that spread to her loins and her limbs, engulfing her with a vulnerability that was completely foreign to her, a vulnerability that reduced her to a mass of needs that begged to be met, desires that not only bordered on the physical, but were tied tightly to the emotional.

She kissed him back, kissed him as if she was never going to be kissed or kiss again. Kissed him as if he could save her from the abyss that loomed before her, lonely and large.

Kissed him as if there was no yesterday, no tomorrow, only now.

Forever.

All of her life, she'd always been the strong one because there was no one else to rely on, nowhere else to turn. She'd been strong because there had been no choice and had learned never to let her barriers down because the consequences were too grave.

But just for tonight, she didn't want to be strong. She wanted to be held and if not loved, then made love to, made love with. If it was all fantasy, all make-believe, then she would deal with it in the harsh morning light. But for now, she needed to have someone with her, someone she could pretend cared.

As he kissed her, his head spinning out of focus, Max slipped his hands to her breasts. Touching the soft flesh filled him with deep, urgent desire that threatened to overpower both of them.

He wanted her, had wanted her possibly from the very first. Because she'd sparked him with her courage, her fire, her determination and go-to-hell attitude. He had never met anyone quite like her. And this frailty he'd uncovered within her...

Abruptly Max reined himself in.

He couldn't take advantage of this vulnerability within her, couldn't take advantage of her. He wasn't his father. The very thought, the very fear that he could be, that he could turn into the very man he'd loathed for so long, had haunted him through all of his adolescent and adult life.

Like some kind of giant roadblock, it had impeded his life.

Fear of turning into his father had kept him from ever becoming serious with any woman he'd been interested in. Because he could not risk the chance that he would ever do to any woman what his father had done to his mother. He'd sworn that on his mother's grave so many years ago. The only way he knew how to keep that promise was to never become involved with a woman for more than a night.

This night, a small voice within him whispered. *Make it this night.*

But he would be thinking only of himself, not of her. And it was her that he was concerned about.

As difficult as it was, as much as he wanted her, Max drew back and looked at Cara's face.

"You're sure?"

Cara didn't want to say anything, didn't want to have to think about it, about anything. She wanted only to drown her thoughts in a river of reaction. Reaction to his kindness, to his masculinity, to the very real, physical pull she felt.

That she had been feeling all along.

Words, thoughts would only ruin the moment. Would only drag reality in. And reality was cold.

"*Shhh,*" was all Cara said as she framed his face with her hands and drew his mouth to hers.

He wanted to stop her, wanted to be sure that she

would have no regrets when this was over, but he had no power to draw on.

She'd drained it all away.

All he wanted to do was make love with her. Until there was no night left. Until the tears on her cheeks had evaporated as if they never existed.

He could feel her heart racing along with his, could feel her breasts rising and falling tantalizingly against his chest. He lost the battle before he ever reached for a sword.

He was hers.

Max didn't remember undressing her, couldn't recall how his own clothes disappeared. All that occurred in a distant, obscure haze. All he was sure of was that she was too hard to resist and he would disintegrate in the fire of his own making if he couldn't have her.

Garments flew off, torn away by an urgency that had seized them both.

He caressed her body as if it was something that wasn't altogether real, but fashioned out of his deepest fantasizes.

Cara felt beautiful to the touch and he longed to touch her, to discover all the places that gave her pleasure, because her pleasure was his.

Max was careful not to go too fast, even though every fiber of his being urged him to. He didn't want to frighten her, wanted to leave a door open, just a crack, no matter what it cost him, for her to be able to pull away if she suddenly changed her mind.

He couldn't take her if she did.

He prayed she wouldn't.

She didn't.

Instead she seemed to be on fire, her body radiating heat at every movement.

When he went slowly, she twisted her body beneath his, tantalizing him, her fingers lightly feathering along his rib cage, his back, his hips.

She had, he realized, absolutely no idea of the power she wielded, no concept of what she could do to a man just by the light press of her lips to his body.

He moaned as she pressed her lips urgently beneath his chin, her tongue lightly gliding along his throat. His arms tightened around her, needs battering at him at every turn.

"A man can only hold back so long," he told her, his breathing heavy, his head and senses filled with the scent of her.

"Then don't." She whispered the invitation against his skin.

The last of his control snapped like a dried twig caught within a raging inferno.

Rolling Cara from him and onto her back, he drew his body over hers. As he kissed her almost senseless, he coaxed her legs apart with his knee, anticipation racing through his body.

And then, watching her eyes for a sign that she suddenly regretted what was happening, seeing only his own features reflected there, Max slowly lowered himself, filling her.

He heard Cara gasp his name, felt her close around him, her body moving seductively.

Max began to move, first slowly, then more urgently as her hips fit against his and mimicked the movement, the harmony that had captured them both and now held them tightly together in its grip.

His heart racing at an ever-increasing tempo, Max threaded his fingers through hers, locking both hands tightly over her head. Reality faded away to less than a pinprick as he drove them over the ridge to a place they both desperately wanted to go.

Chapter 11

She'd screwed up.

Royally.

There was no reason, Cara thought as she quickly pulled on her clothes, for her to have fallen apart like that last night. She'd had that nightmare before, had lived through that nightmare and managed to go on.

Why had she crumbled like some stale, forgotten-about cookie this time?

It was *his* fault. All Ryker's fault for being so damn nice to her.

Gathering up her things in the room, Cara glared at the man who was still asleep in the bed. It was all his fault for sensing exactly what she needed and providing it for her so that she had no control, no anger to fall back on and keep her strong.

Well, she was angry now. Plenty angry. With herself, with him. With the whole damn world.

For two cents, she'd walk out that door and leave him here. She could tell the sheriff that there had been a change in plans and she was going on alone with the prisoner. No reason in the world not to believe her.

Determined, Cara took a step toward the door.

And then stopped.

She sighed. Ryker had given her his word back at the gas station that he wouldn't leave her while she went and changed and he hadn't.

Frustrated, she dragged her hand through her hair, torn. Was her word worth less than his?

No, damn it, it wasn't. It was just that…just… It was understood between them that she wouldn't try to take the prisoner. Was her tacit word less than his?

More angry with herself than ever, she dropped the things she was carrying on the floor and turned back around. Only to find Ryker sitting up in bed, watching her. The blanket was strategically planted on his torso, but not so strategically that it could make her forget or block out the hard body that she damn well knew was just beneath it.

Her mouth suddenly went annoyingly dry.

Max's lips curved in amusement. "Change your mind about leaving?"

She squared her shoulders. There was nothing she hated more than being second-guessed. Or being predictable. "And if I haven't?"

She had. She'd already given herself away by the way she'd hesitated at the door. "You'd be surprised how fast I could get out of this bed and get dressed."

Standing where she was, Cara arched one knowing

brow. "Get lots of practice with irate husbands coming home unexpectedly?"

Max looked at her, trying to figure out what was going on in her head. By the expression on Rivers's face, he judged that she had rebuilt some of the barriers that had been taken down last night.

"I've never made love to anyone's wife," he told her simply.

Cara believed him.

She had no idea why. There was no reason for her to believe that a man who looked the way he did, who despite his chosen profession had raw charm coming out of every pore, would draw the line about the type of willing women he would take to his bed. But she did.

It made him more honorable. She didn't want to like him. It made things harder for her.

"Hooray for you," she said crisply. She looked down at the things she'd dropped, her purse, the small bag with the change of clothes. "We need to get going if we're to stay on schedule."

They were back in their corners, he thought, with an entire boxing ring between them. Maybe it was better that way. Last night she'd opened up a door to things that were better left untouched as far as he was concerned. He didn't like being confronted with feelings that weren't cut-and-dried.

He'd never liked things getting any more complicated than they already were and bringing this prisoner back to his uncle and Montebello was complicated enough for him right now.

"Be right with you, Rivers," he promised, hurrying out of bed. Max heard her suck in her breath and turned toward her, his discarded pants in his hand. Amusement teased his mouth as he looked at her expression. "Something wrong?"

Cara gritted her teeth together. Damn him. Ryker looked even better in the daylight than he had last night. Last night she hadn't really looked, only reacted. The full impact of his body hadn't completely registered.

It did now and she could feel adrenaline beginning to race through her. Could feel color beginning to heat her cheeks.

She turned away, pretending to be impatient. Pretending not to suddenly be getting very, very warm.

"Nothing," she snapped. "Just hurry up. We've still got five hundred miles to cover before we get to Shady Rock and in order to get the bounty, we need to get there before tomorrow."

"Ah, the bounty. Right."

She resented the almost mocking tone he took. Probably didn't know what it meant to do without, she thought. Probably had women paying his way all along.

"Then I guess we'd better get going," he agreed, coming up behind her.

Cara stiffened. He couldn't have possibly gotten dressed that fast. And if he hadn't, if he was standing there behind her in all his glory, she wasn't entirely sure she could make it out the door.

No matter what her feelings were about the rest of it, about what had happened last night, there was no way she could deny that Ryker was one magnificent specimen of manhood.

Cara realized that she was holding her breath just

as he circled around and came to stand in front of her.
The rat was dressed.

Reaching for the door, Max looked at her innocently. "Well?"

Grabbing her things, Cara yanked open the door
and sailed passed him without deigning to give him
so much as a single glance.

They were on the road an hour later. Cara would
have preferred to be gone sooner, but Mrs. Adler had
refused to let either of them leave without making
what she called a small breakfast.

Martha Adler was of the old school and felt that
breakfast was the most important meal of the day—
and the more of it you had, the better. She also insisted on packing a substantial lunch for them "in
case you don't find a good place to stop along the
road."

In less than a couple of hours, Cara felt closer to
Mrs. Adler than she ever had to any of her foster
mothers.

Martha embraced them both before sending them
on their way. Cara knew that it didn't make any sense,
but she felt as if she were leaving behind family.

"Nice woman," Max commented once they were
outside the house.

The sheriff beamed with pride at the compliment.
"The best."

Cara could only agree.

The road from La Cuchara Del Oro to Shady Rock
was marked with sun, heat and huge pockets of si-

lence that the music from the car radio did nothing to dispel.

Because Cara appeared to need to work things through, Max let her take the wheel when they left the sheriff's office with Weber in tow.

He lived to regret it.

She drove like a bat out of hell, taking her aggressions out on the empty road. Small towns whizzed by, mere blurs in the rearview mirror.

As long as the road was level and there were no cars traveling in either direction, he silently argued with himself, they were safe enough—barring a blowout. From either tire or woman, Max qualified.

After two hundred miles had gone by, Max found himself wanting to talk to her, to slowly broach the subject of what had been, he judged for both of them, not a night to carelessly throw away.

But that kind of a discussion, even in part, didn't belong within the confines of a car that was being shared by their mutual prisoner.

So he kept his peace and waited for the journey to be over.

They ate on the road and stopped only twice. Each time Cara got back behind the wheel. He was beginning to think of it as her car.

"Sure you don't want me to take over?" he asked as they got in after the second gas station stop.

Her hands tightened around the wheel and she peeled out. "I'm sure. You've taken over enough."

He knew she wasn't talking about driving, but there as nothing he could do, other than keep his own counsel. For the time being, he did.

She wasn't the only one who needed to work a few things through.

They reached Shady Rock, Colorado, just a hair-breadth before six o'clock in the afternoon. Max looked around as they entered the town. For all the world, it looked almost exactly like half a dozen other towns they had just passed along the road. A general store, a gas station, a diner and a sheriff's office, with several scores of houses and some apartments thrown in for good measure.

It didn't look like much, but he kept that thought to himself, along with everything else he'd wanted to say. At the moment, he didn't feel very diplomatic. He was hot, tired and not exactly in the best of spirits. Beside him, Weber was beyond surly, cursing at them in a language that Max surmised was entirely unfamiliar to Cara.

But not to him.

Cara glanced over her shoulder at Weber after his latest outburst. The papers she had in her purse from the bondsman gave her no particulars on the prisoner's background. All she knew was that he was guilty of burglary.

But she was beginning to suspect that there was more to it. Especially since he was wanted in another country.

"If that guy's real name is Weber," she commented to Max as she pulled his car up in front of the sheriff's office, "I'll eat my hat."

Max got out first and rounded the trunk. No longer handcuffed to the prisoner, he reached in through the partially opened window and unlocked one handcuff from the strap.

"You don't have a hat," he pointed out.

"I'll buy one."

They were home, she thought. There was no feeling of finally having arrived, but this was as much home as any place she'd lived in. Shady Rock was where her travels had brought her. Where her longing for stability had propelled her once she had discovered that the only person who had ever mattered in her life, Bridgette Applegate, had returned here to live out the rest of her years in the house where she had grown up.

Cara had envied Bridgette that, having somewhere to retreat to that contained warm, heartening memories of her childhood. Her own childhood had been scattered across three states and far more towns than she cared to ever remember.

"Got him?" she asked Max.

He held up the handcuff that was now snapped onto his wrist.

She had a flashback from last night, remembering the way his hand had felt along her flesh. Warm, soothing. Gentle.

She shook off the memory and turned on her heel. Leading the way, she breezed into the sheriff's office. The man looked as if he was preparing to go home.

"Hi, Bryce, I've got him. Just like I promised."

Sheriff Bryce Allen looked up from his desk, his prematurely lined face wreathing in a smile once he realized who had walked in. Sharp brown eyes washed over the tall man with her before Bryce turned his attention to the woman he had come to respect a great deal in the last three years. She didn't look the part, but Cara Rivers was the best damn tracker he'd ever come across.

"Knew you'd bring him back, Cara." He rounded his desk, picking up the keys to the cell in the back. "You're like one of those damn Canadian Mounties, except a lot better looking." He winked at her, then glanced toward the tall, thin young woman sitting at the desk on the side. There was a phone with several lines lit on her desk but she was ignoring them, her face buried in a magazine. "Look alive, Alice, time to earn your paycheck and do a little paperwork."

Alice Horton, secretary and chief dispatcher for the Shady Rock Sheriff's Department, tore her gaze away from the story about the latest Hollywood divorce she was reading and looked at the sheriff. She wasn't supposed to call him Uncle Bryce here, although it was that very connection that had landed her this job in the first place.

She also looked, for the first time, at the three people who had entered the office.

The magazine she was reading slid from her limp fingers, falling to the tall, precariously stacked pile of magazines that were tilted haphazardly against her desk. Magazines that dealt with people who led lives that were far more exciting and glamorous than hers.

Her mouth was already hanging open. Somehow, clutching the arms of her chair, Alice somehow managed to rise to her feet.

"You're him." The words dragged themselves across an entirely dried throat. She began to pick up speed. "Tell me you're him. You've got to be him, you look just like him," she all but squealed. Her head swiveled around toward her uncle. "It's him. He's here."

The sheriff had seen her like this before, so starstruck that she was completely incoherent, like the time that country singer's bus broke down right outside of town. She'd been a babbling idiot for more than a week after that.

But as far as he knew, there was no rock star, no movie star within a fifty-mile radius, give or take a few miles.

"Alice, what the hell are you babbling about?"

She pointed one slightly chipped, red-tipped fingernail at Max. She looked at the sheriff incredulously. "Don't you know who he is?"

"Yes," Cara quipped. "A royal pain in the butt."

"Royal," Alice echoed. "He's royal all right." Alice's eyes were in jeopardy of bugging out as she stared at Cara. "How could you not know?"

Cara fished out the handcuff keys and unlocked the cuff that was on Max, snapping it in place around Weber's other wrist instead. She gave the man a push to move him in the sheriff's direction.

"Here, Bryce, put this man in jail so you can sign the papers. I want to collect my money and be on my way," Cara said to the sheriff. "Know what?" she demanded, turning toward Alice.

The woman had always struck her as being more than a little ditzy, her face stuck in a magazine, her head in the clouds. She knew the sheriff kept Alice on despite her lack of professionalism because she was his wife's niece. Bryce was nothing if not loyal, but even he knew that the young woman would have never made it in the real world.

Max frowned. Damn it, he'd have thought that in an out-of-the-way place like Shady Rock, he wouldn't encounter what he was always on his guard against. Being recognized. One look at the young woman's face and Max knew that the charade was up. He'd seen the same starstruck expression ad nauseum before he had finally decided to abandon the merry-go-round he was on and cleave to a life of anonymity across the ocean.

Because the tabloids referred to him by an alliterated nickname he found irritating—the disenchanted duke—and the infernal paparazzi who were pedaling photographs taken of him almost a decade ago, his former life insisted on haunting him and disrupting the life he had made for himself here in the States.

Trying to ignore the adoring stare the receptionist had fixed on him, Max turned toward the sheriff. He had to put in his claim to the prisoner before things blew up in his face.

"Sheriff, I need to speak to you regarding the prisoner."

The sheriff looked at him uncertainly, trying to figure out why Alice looked so loopy. He kept one eye trained on the man Cara had brought in. "What about the prisoner?"

Max glanced at Cara. He could see that she was rapidly becoming annoyed. "It seems that Ms. Rivers and I have equal claim to him."

"I got to him first," Cara insisted, still leery of being aced out of the bounty money. Just because Ryker had been everything she'd needed last night didn't mean that she was going to allow herself to get blindsided by him when it came to the bounty.

Trying to remain impartial, the sheriff shook his head. "Sorry, but as far as I know, there's only one bounty on him and if Cara says she got to him first, then it belongs to her."

As they negotiated, Weber became more and more verbally abusive, while Alice looked as if she was alternating between wanting to jump out of her skin and being struck dumb.

Trying to ignore the latter, Max kept his eye on the former. "It's not about a bounty, it's about getting this man back to Montebello."

"Montebello?" The sheriff wasn't surprised. The mystery of the missing prince had been on TV again recently. Then a man—Tyler Ramsey, if he recalled correctly—had shown up on behalf of the Montebellan authorities, asking about the bail jumper.

Alice finally found her tongue. "That's what I've been trying to tell you. This is Maximillian Sebastiani. The Disenchanted Duke."

She triumphantly held up a magazine, then flipped to the proper page. There was a family layout, taken when Max was thirteen. The year before his mother died.

Seeing the photograph of his mother, sitting serenely beside her husband, bracketed by her sons, made Max's heart ache. He would have given anything if that smile on her face had been genuine, had been merited.

But even as the photograph was being taken, his mother had been dealing with his father's latest infidelity. The man had never made an effort to be discreet. He hadn't cared enough about her feelings to do that.

Pushing herself in front of the sheriff and directly in Max's face, Alice curtsied awkwardly. "Pleased to meet you, Your Highness. I'm Alice Horton."

Taking her hand, he drew the woman to her feet. "I'm not 'Your Highness.' That title is strictly for my uncle."

"Your uncle?" Cara echoed, staring at Max, completely stunned. What the hell was going on here? Just who had she made love with last night?

"The king," Alice told her importantly. She pointed to a man in the background of the photograph. "King Marcus of Montebello."

Looking at the photograph, Cara's eyes grew wide. She looked back at Max. "Your uncle's a king?" This all sounded too implausible for words. Yes, he was charming in a rugged sort of way, but a duke? This had to be some kind of joke.

Trapped, Max had no recourse but to tell the truth. "Yes. It's a small country." He realized that he was apologizing for his identity. He hadn't meant to, but Rivers looked so astonished, and not in a good way, he felt the need to try to smooth things over.

"Kingdom," Alice interjected with a heartfelt sigh, pressing the magazine to her chest, her eyes fastened on Max as if they would never turn elsewhere again. "It's a kingdom."

This was a little too much to digest. The sheriff looked from his niece to the man she was mooning over. "All right. What do you need with regard to this prisoner?"

Without realizing it, Cara fisted her hands on her hips. She glared at Max. He made her feel like a complete idiot. Had he been laughing at her the entire time he'd made love with her?

"Yes, that's what I want to know."

For the moment, Max ignored the furious woman next to him. His duty came first. "My country has a warrant out for this man's arrest and my uncle, King Marcus, would consider it a political favor on the part of your country if you would allow me to bring him back to face official charges in Montebello. There is an extradition treaty in effect. I will bring him back once things are squared away."

But Cara had only heard one thing. "Your country," she jeered. "And here I thought that 'your country' was the U.S."

Max glanced at her, perturbed. Calling Montebello his country had been an unfortunate slip on his part, made necessary by the circumstances. After all, he was representing Montebello in this.

"It is, now," Max clarified. "But I was born in Montebello." He lost the first layer of his patience. "Look, Sheriff, I don't have time to argue about this. I need to return to Montebello with this man as soon as possible."

Rather than let the sheriff answer, Cara broke in. This wasn't acceptable. There was too much at stake. "He's not going anywhere until I get my bounty money."

The money again. It just didn't add up for him. Rivers didn't seem like the obsessively greedy type. But then, maybe he'd misread her. Considering the short time that they'd been thrown together, he couldn't exactly call himself an expert on the woman.

"You'll get your money once the king is finished

with him.'' Provided, he added silently, that it was really that simple. If Weber had had anything to do with the crown prince of Montebello's plane crash and disappearance, the king would never be finished with him. ''You have my word.''

''I don't want your word,'' she informed him tersely, ''I want the money.'' She looked at the sheriff. ''I need it now, Sheriff, and if you don't sign those papers, I won't be getting it. There's a time factor involved. Weber has to be back before tomorrow, noon, otherwise, I forfeit the bounty. Well, he's here. Any deal you make with the duke here is between you, him, the court and the bail bondsman.'' Her tone indicated that she wasn't about to be drawn into the discussion, or budge from her stand. ''Now process the papers for me so I can see Phil about the reward and we'll call it a day.''

Faced with this dilemma, the sheriff knew he couldn't just take the high road or proceed the way he would have wanted to. There were rules to follow, even if he didn't like it. Ruffling a foreign government's feathers was not something he was about to undertake.

''Can't do that, Cara.''

Max saw thunder in her eyes.

''Wait, I have an idea,'' he interjected quickly.

She'd just bet he did.

Chapter 12

Max started to take her arm in order to lead her off to the side, but Cara shrugged him away. Her eyes were cold when she looked at him.

"You can talk without manhandling me."

What the hell was she talking about? "Rivers, I'm just trying to take you aside."

"Fine."

Cara moved to the side of the room of her own volition. She didn't want him touching her, didn't want to run any risk of being swayed by the mere pressure of his hand. He'd already done too much damage to her last night as it was.

Part of her had actually begun to believe he was a good guy, and then he pulled this stunt on her. She should have known he was no different than the rest. Ryker, or whatever he called himself, was just setting her up.

Well, if he thought she was going to bow down before his wishes like some little dandelion in the wind, he was in for a shock.

Cara glared as she swung around to face him. "Talk," she ordered.

A man could get frostbite from a glare like that. Maybe he had it coming, Max thought. "I'll write you a check for the ten thousand."

Whatever she expected him to say, it wasn't this. "You'll do what?"

"Write you a check for the ten thousand," Max repeated.

She didn't believe him. This had to be a trick, a set-up of some kind. "In what? Montebellan Monopoly money?"

He laughed shortly. "We don't have Monopoly over there and the check will be payable in American money. I have a bank account in Los Angeles."

Some of her anger abated as she tried to make sense of the offer. "Why would you do that?"

It was the look in her eyes that did it, but he knew saying that would only have him falling into a fresh cauldron of trouble. In the interest of peace, he grasped at the most logical explanation.

"Because you did catch Weber fair and square and because I don't have the time to argue over this. The sooner I get him to Montebello, the sooner I can return him."

If, indeed, he could return him, Max added silently. More than likely, the crimes that "Weber" had committed in Montebello were more heinous than the one he was charged with in the U.S. Then he knew he wouldn't be able to return Weber. And even if he could return the man, as Rivers had already pointed out, if she didn't have Weber in jail by tomorrow morning, she wasn't eligible to collect the bounty. Since the money seemed to mean so much to her, it was only fair that she should get it.

There was still suspicion in her eyes, as if she was waiting for him to spring something on her. "You'd do that?"

"Yes."

She didn't know of anyone who had that kind of money to throw around just because they felt guilty about what they were doing.

"If you're that well-off, what are you doing playing private eye—" Her eyes narrowed. "Or was that a lie, too?"

"No, that wasn't a fabrication." He deliberately avoided the word lie. "I am a licensed private investigator." Max reached for his wallet. "I can show you my license."

She waved him away. If the man was a good liar, he would have covered that base as well. Besides, she didn't need to see anything, bogus or authentic. What mattered was the bounty, or its equal.

"All right, I'll take the check." Cara fixed him with a warning look. "And if it bounces, I'll hunt you down and you know I can do that."

The grin was spontaneous. "Yes, I know you can do that."

Max turned back to the sheriff, who watched them calmly. His secretary made enough fuss for both of them. Leaning over to hear as much of the conversation between him and Rivers as she could, Alice looked as if she were in danger of falling.

"All right, Sheriff, we've come to an agreement. I'll have the proper authorities notify you regarding the legalities concerning transferring custody of the prisoner to Montebello. I'll be taking him back with me."

The sheriff nodded. "Fine. Send your paperwork so that the lawyers and whoever'll be satisfied. As for me, I've got only one stipulation, Duke." He grinned. "Makes me feel like I'm talking to John Wayne. They called him the Duke, you know."

Max nodded. "So I've heard. What's your stipulation?"

The soft brown eyes shifted toward Cara. "That she goes with you to Montebello."

Max stared at the sheriff, stunned. "What?"

Alice looked on wistfully, wishing that there was some reason that she could be sent along instead, or at least as well.

Cara's mouth dropped open. There was no way she wanted to go anywhere with this man, much less leave the country. As far as she was concerned, her job was done. "Me?"

"Yes, you." He'd been sheriff long enough to know an argument when he saw one coming and wouldn't let her protest until he said his piece. "I want that guy back to pay for what he did here. The man tried to break into the Chambers' ranch house. We can't have things like that going on. Things like that have got to be made right. Now, we may look like some backwater hick place to you, Duke, but backwater or not, we've got rules. One of those rules is that if you do something wrong, you're going to have to pay for it. Now Cara here's the one person that I know'll bring him back once the smoke clears.'' He smiled at Cara, meaning every word as a compliment. ''She's like a pit bull.''

She frowned. She'd had better compliments in her time. ''Thank you.''

The sheriff saw nothing wrong in his assessment. ''Don't mention it.'' He motioned to the cell phone that Max had just taken out of his pocket. ''Now, you conclude your business any way you feel you have to, but if Cara doesn't go with you to that place of yours, neither does Weber.'' To get his point across, he adjusted his gun belt. ''And I am the law here.''

Max paused for a moment, thinking. This put a new wrinkle in things. But none that he felt particularly alarmed over. He glanced at Cara. The woman, he noted, didn't exactly looked ecstatic at the turn of events.

''It's all right with me if it's all right with Rivers.''

Oh, no, he wasn't going to put this on her shoulders. She didn't want to go with him, especially after he'd neglected to mention some important facts about his identity. But if he thought she was going to go hide in some corner with hurt feelings, or let him get away with Weber, well, surprise. She wasn't.

''I don't see where I have much choice in the matter,'' she said slowly, ''seeing as how I'm beholden to the sheriff.''

It was the sheriff, at the behest of Bridgette, who he had a great deal of respect for, who had gotten her the job with Phil in the first place. On his own, Phil would have never taken her seriously as a bounty hunter. ''All right, write that check, Ryker, excuse me, Duke,'' she corrected sarcastically. ''I just need enough time to see someone just outside of town and then I'm ready to go wherever I have to.''

Digging into his pocket, Max took out his check-book. "Shall I make it out to you?" It was a rhetorical question. He'd fully expected her to say yes as he reached for a pen on the sheriff's desk. Alice quickly thrust her own pen into his hand, accompanied with a wistful smile. "Thank you."

Alice sighed.

"No," Cara said just as he was about to start writing. They were pressed for time. If it was in her name, she would have to deposit it before she could write a comparable check for Bridgette. "Make it out to Bridgette Applegate."

Max looked at her. "Who?"

"Never mind who." Cara pointed to the opened checkbook. "Just do it." She gave Max the proper spelling of the nurse's first name, aware that the sheriff was looking at her.

Bryce beamed at her as he squeezed her shoulder. "That's a mighty decent thing you're doing, Cara."

She shrugged as Max tore the check off and handed it to her. Folding it, she placed it into her own wallet, then stuffed it into her back pocket.

"I owe Bridgette more than this." She looked at Max. There was curiosity in his eyes, but that was his problem, not hers. She didn't have to bare her soul to him any more than she already had. "You do what you have to do. I'll be back soon."

To her surprise and dismay, Max shook his head. "The plane can't be here before morning."

She'd thought they were going to drive to the Denver airport. He made it sound as if something was coming to their doorstep. "Plane?"

"Montebello is next to Cyprus," he told her. "It takes time for a plane to get here."

"You have your own plane." Even as she said it, she realized it was no longer a question, just a clarification. Just how rich were dukes in this countrylet of his? "Why am I not surprised?"

"It's my uncle's plane," Max explained. "I just know he wouldn't want the prisoner flown back via a commercial airline."

"Heaven forbid he or you be subjected to airline food."

"I was thinking more along the lines that Weber might try to escape and my uncle wouldn't want to put innocent people in jeopardy."

Chagrined, she shrugged carelessly, looking away. "Whatever." Waving at the sheriff, she crossed to the front door.

Max shadowed her steps. "Mind if I tag along? Maybe, while we wait, you can show me the sights."

The only sight she wanted to show him at this moment was the back of a door—slamming in his face.

"You already saw most of them on the way in." Max accompanied her to the parked car. A car, she reminded herself, that was his. If she was going to make it to Bridgette's at a decent time, she needed a car. His. The reason she'd rented a car to begin with when she'd gone after Weber was that her own had been in an accident and she didn't have enough to cover the repairs for it yet. "Oh, all right, suit yourself."

He opened the passenger door. Since she knew

where she was going and he didn't, he saw no point in being the one to drive.

"Warm invitation."

"You want warm?" she shot back, peeling out of the spot and making a complete one-eighty turn with a painful screech. "Get a sweater."

She'd all but thrown him into the driver's seat with that turn, but he said nothing. She needed to work this out of her system. He looked at the cell phone that was still in his hand, but held off calling his uncle. A few minutes one way or another wasn't going to matter.

Cara took another turn, sending him ricocheting to the other side despite his seat belt. If she wasn't careful, she was going to kill them both. "Did I miss something here? Why are you so angry?"

As if the idiot had to ask. Fuming, she tightened her hands on the wheel. "I don't like being lied to."

He'd been very careful there. "No one lied to you."

"Oh?" Where she came from, holding back pertinent information was as good as lying. "Then why didn't you tell me who you really were?"

"That's not lying," he pointed out, "that's just not talking about myself. Most women like men who don't go on about themselves."

He was playing with words. She bet he was good at that, Cara thought. But it would take a lot more than that to snow her. "There's a difference between bragging and saying, 'oh, excuse me, but when you cut me, I bleed blue blood.'"

Humor curved his mouth. He realized that intentionally or not, Cara made him smile a lot. "It's red."

Immersed in her anger, it took her a second to process what he'd just said. "What?"

"My blood," he clarified, "it's red."

Cara blew out a breath. He was doing it again. Duke or not, she was beginning to think of the man as a con artist, the kind that could twist out of any situation and fall into a mud puddle and come out smelling like a rose. "You know what I mean."

Yes, he knew what she meant. Max grew serious, wanting to clear the air once and for all. He was going to be flying with this woman and he didn't want her shooting daggers at him.

"Look, I wasn't lying to you, I was just trying to live a normal life."

What a crock. Couldn't he do any better than that? She spared him a long, disbelieving look. "And chasing after some lowlife for the king of Montebello is normal," she hooted.

It was all in the perspective. "More normal than being a duke. Besides, I don't use the title."

"Alice Groupie thinks you do."

He laughed at the nickname she'd just awarded the secretary. "My younger brother Lorenzo's the duke. I walked away from that life when my father died."

Turning down the block, she looked at him in mild surprise. "Why would you do that? Most people would kill to live that kind of life."

So he'd heard. The grass was always greener when you didn't have to walk through it.

"Most people have no idea what that kind of life is like." For her benefit, he gave her a minitour into his life. "It means being in a fishbowl, never having a private moment to yourself. It means having your every move under almost constant scrutiny. Photographers popping up out of bushes. Never knowing if someone is talking to you or to your lineage.'' He frowned, remembering. Glad to have it all behind him. ''There's nothing genuine about it.''

Cara turned his words over in her head. He sounded so serious, she believed him. Maybe that made her a fool. She didn't know. With a short laugh, she shook her head. It was a small world. ''So I guess in a way, you're a runaway, too.''

Max's protest died before it was spoken. She was right. ''I guess I am at that.''

Who would have ever thought they actually had something in common? When she looked at him, there was a hint of a smile on her lips. A genuine one. ''This is like the *Prince and the Pauper,* except that we don't look alike.''

He thought of last night. ''And the prince never made love to the pauper.''

''No, I don't think the censors would have let Mark Twain get away with that.'' He could still be putting her on, but she didn't think so. ''All right, I guess I see your point.''

''Good.'' That out of the way, he looked at the lonely stretch of road before them. ''So where are we going?''

''To see the woman who saved my life.'' Cara didn't have to look at him to know there was a question coming. The man knew too much about her as it was. ''Don't you have a phone call to make?''

Way ahead of her, Max was already pressing numbers on the keypad.

Though it was the king's private line, he still had

to go through his uncle's personal secretary, Albert, before he was allowed to speak to the man himself. Several minutes lapsed before he heard his uncle's voice. As succinctly as possible, Max filled him on the pertinent details. Leaving out the part about Cara coming along as well.

He could feel her looking at him, waiting for him to drop the bombshell. He kept it at bay.

"I knew I could count on you, Max." His uncle sounded well pleased. "I will have the plane ready to leave within the half hour. I've had it fueled up ever since I called you." There were few men whose abilities and integrity he trusted as implicitly as his oldest nephew's. "Once you arrive, you'll spend a few days with me at the palace, of course."

He hadn't gone into any of the conditions that came along with the extradition. That was best said face-to-face. Though he loved his uncle, he had little desire to see his former homeland. But he couldn't very well refuse the invitation. Besides, he did have to take the prisoner back.

"Yes, of course." He paused. "Uncle, there're complications."

"Oh?"

Though this was not any dark secret, Max still hesitated elaborating even a little. The lines were not secure. "I'll explain when I get there."

Marcus sensed there was more than a minor problem involved. "But you *are* bringing Weber."

Weber. Again, he doubted that was truly the man's name, even though the Wanted poster Cara had shown him bore that alias.

"Yes, I'm bringing the man you sent me for."

Marcus appreciated the wording. His nephew was a smart man.

"Wonderful. Then I shall see you some time late tomorrow." There was a pause, and then the king said, "You've done well, Max."

Max wasn't all that sure if he deserved the king's praise when he terminated the connection.

Cara waited until she was sure the conversation was over. "You didn't tell him I was coming."

Max slipped the phone into his pocket. "You'll be a surprise."

"Great." Sarcasm dripped from her voice. "I love surprising people." They'd been traveling along a road that bordered a small farm. She drove toward the small, two-storied farmhouse. "Well, here we are." Turning off the engine, she pulled up the hand brake. "You can stay in the car if you like, this shouldn't take too long."

He was already getting out of the car. "All the same to you, I'd like to tag along."

Cara shook her head. "I was afraid you'd say that." She couldn't very well tell him not to, seeing as it was his car she'd used and his check in her purse. Resigned, she led the way to the door and rang the bell.

The sound of a dog barking in the background echoed back to them moments before the front door opened.

A frail-looking, gray-haired woman in a plain dress and sensible shoes stood behind the screen door. When she smiled, her face lit up. He liked her instantly.

"Hush, Brutus," she chided the old hound dog, "it's just Cara."

As Max looked on, the woman embraced Cara, then looked at him with bright blue eyes that glowed with unabashed interest. But, unlike the look on the sheriff's secretary's face, he didn't feel as if he was being invaded or his life breached.

"And a friend," the woman told the dog, releasing Cara. "Be on your best behavior," she called over her shoulder to the animal that was even now trotting over to the door. "Brutus doesn't bite," she told Max. "He just likes to frighten people with his bark."

Max looked at Cara, amused. "You and Brutus have a lot in common."

Cara's smile was instant, wide and not entirely genuine. "Yeah, but I bite and don't forget it."

The woman looked at her somewhat uncertainly. "Cara?"

Cara gestured toward Max. "This is—" Stumped, she looked at him. "What do I call you?"

"Max," Max said to the older woman. Taking her hand, he raised it to his lips and kissed it in the courtly fashion he'd been raised.

Bridgette was charmed. "Nice smile," she commented to Cara.

"Yes, it is," Cara agreed. "Covers a myriad of flaws." Though she would have liked to have stayed the evening, she knew that Bridgette would go all out, cooking a meal and making them at home and the woman needed her rest. "We can't stay, Bridgette. I just wanted to stop by and give you this." She placed the check Max had given her into the other woman's hand and folded her fingers over it. "For the farm."

Bridgette looked down at the check, her mouth falling open. She tried to give it back to Cara, but the latter stepped back. "I can't accept this, child."

"Yes," Cara insisted firmly, "you can. I wish it was more, but at least it'll keep those bankers in their cages for a while."

Bridgette pressed her lips together to keep the sudden sob that rose in her throat back. She'd already made her peace with foreclosure. This was like an unexpected miracle.

"This'll pay the back taxes," she said, nodding her head. And then she shook it, looking at the young woman she had taken in so long ago. "Cara, I don't know what to say."

"Don't say anything. Not to me. Just tell those bankers to go—chase themselves." It was clearly not what she wanted to say, but she was tempering her words in deference to the woman before her.

She looked more closely at the check and was puzzled. Had Cara entered into some sort of bargain because of her? "Why is his signature on it?"

Cara waved away the concern she saw in Bridgette's face. How like her to worry about everyone but herself. "Long story. It's in lieu of the bounty money he's acing me out of. The bail jumper I was after is wanted in Montebello and Max needs to take him there before the guy faces the charges against him here."

"I see." She didn't, but she left legal matters to the people around her. Tears filled her eyes as she thought of the breathing space this gave her. The crops she was hoping on would now be able to come in. "I can't tell you what this means to me."

"You don't have to." Impulsively Cara hugged the woman. "Need me to take you into town?"

The bank was closed now, but she could go tomorrow. "No, Elliot'll do that," she assured Cara, referring to her hired hand. "You've done more than enough already." She ran her hand over Cara's hair affectionately. Remembering. "Best thing I ever did in my life was bring you home for chicken soup."

"Chicken soup?" Max asked as they walked back to his car.

"It was more than that." And more than she was willing to go into now. Cara got into the car. "Bridgette's a nurse, retired now. When I met her, I was sick, she took care of me."

He was waiting for more, but it didn't come. "That's pretty sparse on the details."

She shrugged, staring up the car. "Maybe if the plane ride gets too long and we get bored, I'll fill you in." Big maybe, she added silently.

Which meant that for now, she didn't want to discuss it, Max thought.

He of all people understood not wanting to touch the past. The problem was, her past was beginning to interest him.

Possibly more than it should have.

Chapter 13

Max studied Cara's profile as she drove them back to Shady Rock. The woman amazed him. She'd done what appeared to be an entirely selfless act and she wasn't even talking about it. There were some people he knew of back in Montebello who would do well to take a page from her book.

"You made her very happy."

Cara felt a deep sense of satisfaction. The only thing that marred it was that she wished it could have somehow been more. But it would be. There was always another bail jumper to pursue, another bounty to collect. She intended to share the proceeds with Bridgette until the woman was well on her feet again.

"Bridgette deserves to be happy. All she's got is that farm. Woman spent most of her life helping others in one way or another. Never had time for a personal life of her own. Now she's getting on in years and there's no one to look out for her."

"So you do."

It wasn't a question. There was a great deal more to this woman who cleaved to bounty hunting in order to make her living than he'd first thought. She wasn't all noise and bravado.

But then, he had figured that out when they'd made love.

Cara shrugged, dismissing the subject. She didn't like calling attention to her softer, more sentimental side. That was for private moments to be shared with people she trusted. So far, that really only meant Bridgette.

She looked at the road before her and thought about what lay ahead. They were going to be in town pretty soon. "All right, so now what?"

"Well, the king's private plane won't be here until tomorrow around ten." The sheriff had mentioned an airstrip not far out of town. Max left details like that to the king's personal pilot. Roark would find it even if it was little more than square clearing. "So I guess what I need to do is find a place to stay overnight. What's the hotel like?"

There was one hotel over on the other side of town. She'd heard it was nice enough.

"Wouldn't know. I've never stayed there." Cara pressed her lips together, the way he'd noticed she did when she was battling with a thought. "It's a ways down the highway. Probably not grand enough for a duke."

There was that stigma again, he thought, the one that always came up whenever anyone knew his background. People ceased to be comfortable, to be natural, around him. As if he had been part of the court of Ivan the Terrible.

"I don't require grand," Max said mildly. "Just a bed with a pillow and sheets."

"They can supply that." Cara pressed her lips together again. Damn it, the best thing she could do was just leave this alone. Let him go to the hotel, what difference could it make?

Even so, she heard herself saying, "So can I."

The quietly worded offer surprised him. "Is that an invitation?"

She shrugged carelessly, uncomfortable if he was putting any sort of deeper meaning into the act. Uncomfortable with the thought that she was putting any kind of meaning into the act.

Feeling cornered, she gave him an explanation more for her own sake than for his. "You wrote the check, I guess the least I can do is give you a place to stay and a hot meal."

Another surprise. "You cook?" He couldn't really envision Cara doing anything else besides ordering takeout.

"Yes, I cook." She smothered her immediate "raised-hackles" response. There was no point in getting upset over an assumption that, all things considered, was perfectly logical, given her personality. Besides, it was almost true. She wasn't exactly in line to having her own cooking show.

She slanted a glance in his direction. "I said the meal would be hot, I didn't say it would be good."

He laughed. "I'm easy. Hot is good."

And it was, Max thought, looking at her.

The trouble was, it seemed to be getting hotter between them all the time and he didn't think that either one of them was ready for that or really knew what to make of it.

"Then it is true, just as I've suspected. I'm glad you've come to me with this."

King Marcus frowned as he moved around his lavishly sculpted gardens. This was the only place he felt that it was safe enough to conduct a private meeting with anyone. And this meeting was very private. There were only two people in it, himself and Hassan, the son of the very man he had, until recently, been feuding with, Sheik Ahmed.

There was now a truce, reached between two grieving fathers who had each reportedly lost a son. Ahmed's had been found, returning to the arms of the woman he loved, Marcus's daughter, Julia. The two were joined now, by their love and their infant son.

All appeared to be well now between the two countries, but there were those who wished it otherwise. Those who wanted to perpetuate another feud, undermine both governments and seize power.

Because of that, affairs had to be conducted in secret and people kept in the dark.

Dark.

It was the dark that was the problem. Or, more specifically, the Brothers of Darkness. It was a terrorist group that had originated within Sheik Ahmed's own country, Tamir, and had dedicated itself to obliterating anyone, Montebellan, Tamiran or anyone else who did not wholeheartedly agree with them and pledge their life to the cause.

It was the Brothers who had set off a bomb in San

Sebastion, the capital of Montebello, the Brothers who he suspected were behind Lucas's disappearance.

"Yes," Hassan confirmed solemnly. He said what Marcus had already suspected, why he had sent Max to bring Jalil Salim back. The young future sheik looked around the area that was surrounded with green hedges. Just enough for privacy, not enough to hide someone if they approached.

"Jalil Salim, who is passing himself off as this Kevin Weber in the United States, is part of the Brothers of Darkness. According to my father's intelligence agents, he has gone to the United States to try to raise money for the organization. Accordingly he has helped to set up a petroleum business in Texas which is actually a front for this heinous group."

Hassan's frown mirrored the one on the face of the man who had received him. "I do not have to tell you that such an organization, once rooted, can spread, infecting so many other places. The Brothers of Darkness would grow stronger, their organization jeopardizing the governments in both of our countries. They have to be stopped before this happens," he concluded passionately.

Marcus wholeheartedly agreed. With the Brothers of Darkness working within Tamir and the United States, he knew his own country would be particularly vulnerable. He would have an enemy at both flanks. And America was as much the land of opportunity for the dark of heart as it was for the pure. Perhaps even more so.

But since this was a courtesy call from the sheik, Marcus left the arena opened to Ahmed's son. The evil had sprung up within the borders of Tamir and as such, it was their problem. Protocol did not allow for him to intrude unless invited.

"Since Jalil and his men are all natives of your country, how does your father wish to handle this situation?" Unable to contain himself, wanting the problem dealt with swiftly, Marcus began, "I could—"

But Hassan raised a hand, respectfully calling a halt to anything the king was going to propose.

"There is already a plan, Your Highness. My father is sending me to Texas to see about 'negotiating—'" he smiled at the use of the word "—a possible business merger with this so-called up-and-coming petroleum company. Once I am on the inside, I will be in a position to learn more. In the meantime, I was told that you have dispatched Maximillian to bring this scum of the earth back to Montebello."

Marcus tread lightly along the so recently reconstructed bridge between his country and Hassan's. "I have it on good authority that Salim is responsible for several terrorist acts within Montebello and may very well have had a hand in the explosion that ripped apart my son's plane—"

Hassan nodded, his dark eyes growing sympathetic. "Our two families have both had much to grieve over in the last year, Your Highness. But as someone once said, that which does not kill us—"

"—makes us strong," Marcus concluded.

And his father's heart had felt heavy enough at times to have wished for death. But his country needed him at its helm, now more than ever, and the luxury of giving up, of surrendering to the burdens of life, was not his to partake.

The two men shook hands in silence, sealing a political alliance as well as a personal one.

Salim would be in Montebello in less than two days. They could go forward from there.

Max followed Cara into the small, one-story house and looked around the surrounding area. Vaulted, wooden beamed ceilings met his eye. The living room appeared to be both large and cozy at the same time. Two things at once. Much the way its owner was, Max mused.

"So this is where you live?"

She swung around, immediately on the defensive. "What's wrong with it?"

"Nothing." He had no idea where that wary tone she'd used had come from. He certainly hadn't done anything to bring it on. "You know, you really should do something about that tendency you have to see battlefields where there are only meadows."

She tried to remember if there was something in her refrigerator that she could safely offer a guest. She'd been away for several weeks and all she knew she had were two boxes of cereal in the pantry. Any milk had long since turned sour.

"Meadows can be turned into battlefields in the blink of an eye." Moving around several jars of spaghetti sauce, she located a box of spaghetti. Dinner, she thought in triumph. She glanced at him over her shoulder. "Ever hear of Bull Run?"

He thought for a moment. "No."

"Sorry, I forgot." Closing the pantry door with her elbow, she brought the jar of sauce and box of spaghetti to the counter. "You're not American."

"I am in part." He watched her take a pot out of the closet and search for another. Something stirred inside of him. Since when had rummaging for cookware become sexy? "My mother was born in this country. In California."

If she'd had a palace to live in, she damn well wouldn't have left it. Cara filled one pot with water and placed it on her stove.

"So that's what you're doing in California? Looking for your roots?"

More like escaping them, he thought. "Something like that."

She turned the heat up under the pot and then placed the second one on the burner. "Did your mother come with you?"

"No," he said quietly. "She died when I was fourteen."

That was too soon to lose a mother, but at least he'd had a mother for a while. She had no idea what hers had even looked like.

Picking up a can opener, Cara turned it upside down and placed the tip under the lid, maneuvering it so that she could get air under the seal. A small popping noise announced her success. She remembered he'd said his father was dead, too. "That makes you an orphan, too. I guess that gives us something else in common."

She twisted the lid off and dumped the contents of the jar into the second pot. Max took both the jar and lid and tossed them away for her in the trash can.

"Orphans and runaways. Not the most positive things to build on."

She looked at him sharply. "Who says we're building anything?"

He moved a little closer to her. "Would you be that averse to a friendship?"

She suddenly made herself very busy. Nerves began to move just under the surface.

"You in California, me here." She took out two dinner plates from the cupboard. "Don't see that there'd be much point in starting anything, friendship or otherwise."

She was nervous, he suddenly realized. The idea made him smile. "Our paths might cross. Our lines of work keep us moving around."

He was standing much too close to her, standing in her space, taking up her air. Reminding her of things that were best left forgotten. "And you had just better keep moving, mister, because—"

He took the ladle out of her hand and placed it on the counter. "Because why, Cara?"

Was it just her, or was the air slightly thicker? Harder to breathe? "There you go, using my name again. I like it better when you call me Rivers."

He looked at her, his curiosity definitely aroused. "Why?"

Why was her mouth suddenly so dry and her fingertips tingling? He was just a man, nothing more. Why did the room seem to be tilting just because he was in it? "Because when you call me that, there's a professional space between us."

"And you want space." Rather than move back, he seemed to move forward without moving an inch.

"Yes." She damned her voice for quavering over the single word.

Max looked into her eyes, an indulgent smile on his lips. "Now who's lying?"

She felt a flash of anger and quickly rallied around it, vainly attempting to make it her standard. "Look, just because I slept with you once doesn't mean I'm about to hop into the sack with you every time we're in a room alone together."

"No hopping," he promised.

His eyes already seemed to be making love to her. *Were* making love to her. And definitely undermining her resolve. She tried to make him understand. "I slept with a private investigator, not a duke."

Max shook his head, his eyes keeping her prisoner. "You slept with a man, not a vocation."

Didn't he understand? She'd been on equal footing before, but here she was out of her league. "Being a duke isn't a vocation, it's a way of life. You're used to grand things—"

"Yes," he said softly, feathering his fingers through her hair, his eyes caressing her. "I am."

She felt herself weakening and sinking fast. "Damn it, you don't play fair, Ryk—what the hell do I call you, anyway?"

Max reached behind her and turned off the burner beneath the pot of water. "'Max' always worked."

She was determined to be defiant until what she now realized was the inevitable end. "I like Ryker better."

His smile got under her skin with long, arousing fingers. "Then use Ryker if it makes you comfortable. I want you to be comfortable, Cara."

She knew better. He was a man. There was only

one thing a man wanted a woman to be. "You want me to be naked."

He laughed, but only softly. Seductively. She was beginning to think she hadn't a chance. "Eventually. Getting there is half the fun."

"Fun?" she breathed, feeling everything beginning to turn upside down.

"Fun. Pleasure," Max supplied, gently beginning to tease the first button on her blouse out of its hole. "Use any word you want." He separated another button from its hole. "But use it later. Because I need to kiss you now."

She had to swallow before she spoke. The words were sticking in her throat. "Need?"

"Yes," Max whispered, his lips almost touching hers. "Need."

It was the word that defined what she was feeling as well. Need. A huge, overpowering need that quickly ate through her like a hungry shrew, chewing away at all the walls of resistance she was so vainly trying to reconstruct.

The last time they had been made of steel, and still they had crumbled. This time, they were hardly as strong as papier-mâché.

Because she had made love with him.

Because she knew how tender he could be.

She was drowning in her own needs. Cara told herself that what he was saying, what he was doing to her, was all a ruse. Men like Ryker knew how to play women, knew how to make them want what wasn't any good for them. It didn't matter, she couldn't convince herself. Couldn't pull away from him.

She wanted it as much as he did. Maybe even more, though she hated to admit it, even to herself.

But this was good for her, she argued silently. However fleeting, however invisible its foundations were, this wild, heady feeling, this rush of adrenaline and desire, was good for her.

It amazed Max that the fire he felt inside his loins and belly was even greater this time around than it had been the last. It was his experience that mysteries that had been breached were not as tempting the second time around. Somehow, that didn't seem to be the case this time around.

She was still a mystery to him, still an unsolved puzzle. They were dancing to a tune that was unfamiliar to him. Unlike other women in his life, Cara wasn't eager to please him, wasn't eager to be with him every waking moment, and yet despite this, or perhaps because of this, he found her fascinating. And heady.

Like alcohol consumed on a stomach too empty to offer any resistance.

Just as her head went spinning out of control and her knees threatened to buckle humiliatingly, Max surprised her by scooping her up in his arms.

Drawing her lips back from his, she looked at him, a question in her eyes.

He gave voice to his. "Where's your bedroom?"

The feel of his breath on her skin excited her. "There." She pointed off into the distance, her sense of direction all but stripped away from her, along with what she'd once thought was her common sense. "Why?"

"Because—" he pressed a kiss to her throat "—if

I don't get you there in the next five seconds, I'm going to make love to you right here on the floor.''

Make love.

Not have sex, make love.

Cara wrapped herself up in the word, pretending it was real. That he meant exactly that. She had never heard the word applied to her. No one had ever told her they loved her.

Just for now, with her heart swelling in anticipation, she pretended that someone had.

Trying not squirm as a myriad of delicious feelings battled for control of her body, Cara pressed a kiss to his neck.

"I like the floor," she whispered, feeling decadent and wildly innocent at the same time. He made her feel an entire spectrum of diverse, opposing emotions and it was wonderful.

The next moment, as a rush of adrenaline pulsated and surged through his veins, Max set her back on the floor. Her arms wound around his neck, rejecting a separation.

She wanted him. Here and now. Wanted this man right here on her rug.

She was a tigress, there was no other way to describe her. On some distant plane, Max had thought he knew what to anticipate, at least as far as the physical mechanics of lovemaking went.

He was wrong.

This time, if anything, she was the one who took charge. She was the one to make love to him. Though he had made the first move by beginning to unbutton her blouse, it was she who began to undress him.

Her fingers flew nimbly, teasingly over the buttons

on his shirt, undoing them one by one, pressing a kiss to his chest each time a little more skin appeared. She drew the shirttails out of his waistband and then pulled the material from his shoulders, all but ripping it off his arms.

Flinging the shirt behind her, Cara unnotched his belt, then flicked apart the snap to his jeans. Jeans on a duke. The world was a funny place.

Her mouth curved.

Her eyes were wicked as she looked into his. Hypnotizing him. And then her fingers began to delve beneath the barriers of the material, slowly slipping down to touch his flesh. Making him quicken with anticipation, making him groan as just the barest hint of the tips of her fingers skimmed along the length of him.

She was making him crazy.

Gripping her shoulders, Max pulled her to him, sealing his mouth to hers. Feasting on her lips.

Making love to her face, her limbs, her very being.

A voice within his brain cautioned him to go slow, but it was merely a vague, almost muted hum somewhere in the background.

He didn't listen. He didn't want to.

His hands flew over her body, divesting her of her clothes quickly, hardly able to hold back the raging hunger he felt eating away at him. Quickly, as he caressed her, he rediscovered what he already knew was there.

Finding her for the first time.

Again.

If possible, her body was even more magnificent this time around than it had been the last. He touched, caressed, tantalized, worshiped. And with each pass, he discovered that he couldn't get enough of her.

Every kiss gave birth to another, more urgent than the last.

He hardly recognized himself, but there was no time for thought, for analysis. There was only time to react, to savor.

To make love.

Bringing her as gently as he could to the floor, his body poised over hers, he momentarily pulled back, looking at her. Memorizing the features that his fingers had already committed to memory.

"You're magnificent," he whispered.

His mouth over hers, he gave her no time to respond. No time to think. He took her because she was already his. And he was already hers.

Chapter 14

Afterglow, Cara discovered, had staying power. It was still with her the next morning as she boarded King Marcus's private jet, a luxurious Gulfstream. Her body throbbed like a timpani drum solo every time she thought of the night she'd shared with Max.

They'd made love three times. On the living-room floor, on her bedroom floor and then in her bed. Exhausted, contented, she'd finally fallen asleep in his arms, which to her was even more intimate than the lovemaking. It meant that on some level, some part of her trusted him.

She didn't want to. Because trusting someone meant giving up her defenses. It meant surrendering and being left completely exposed.

She didn't seem to have a choice.

Last night, the dream, the nightmare, hadn't come. It was as if, subconsciously, she'd felt that there was someone to protect her now.

But that in itself, was a dream. A fantasy. This affair had no future. How could it? Max was someone whose lineage could be traced back for dozens of generations, planted in the garden of a country she'd never even really been aware of until just a few days ago.

Her lineage stopped with her. The only person who she felt was part of her family wasn't even related to her by blood. Instead it was a woman who had taken her under her wing and into her heart.

What sort of future did that give them? The answer was simple. None.

And yet...

And yet, she wanted desperately to go on pretending that, based on yesterday, there was a tomorrow for the two of them.

Cara looked out the window at the endless clear sky that stretched out before her, searching for a sense of tranquillity, however fleeting.

She supposed, in the literal sense of the word, there was a tomorrow for them. Tomorrow and the day after and the day after that until she finally returned with Weber to American soil. And then she and Max would part company.

They might even part company now, she thought. After all, once his king was done with Weber, there was no need for Max to hurry back to the States. Maybe he would decide to stay in his native country for a while. Absence did make the heart grow fonder. Maybe now that he had something to compare it to, Montebello would seem better to him.

But she had a life waiting for her in Shady Rock, such as it was. And she would have to leave.

"You're awfully quiet," Max commented. Weber was in the small cargo compartment, guarded by two of the soldiers that his uncle had sent over along with the Gulfstream. Max could afford to sit back and relax. And study the woman sitting in the seat beside him. She'd been pensive for a long while now. "What are you thinking about?"

That this is going to be over soon. "That I hate plane rides."

Flying had been part of his life for as far back as Max could remember. One of his first memories was sitting beside his mother as they went on a royal visit to see Queen Elizabeth II of England. Getting around by plane was almost second nature to him. He'd never given it much thought.

"There's nothing to worry about," he assured her. "It's safer than driving a car."

She'd heard that before and wasn't sold. "Never heard of a car falling out of the sky."

The wisecrack, he noted, was without its customary bite. Something was bothering her. Something she didn't want to discuss.

"You're safe, trust me."

Trust me. There it was again, the call to surrender, to give up who she was—a woman who had built in so many safeguards in her life against getting hurt, she was completely swept up in the mechanics and had entirely forgotten how to feel.

Until the other night.

Whether he meant to or not, Max had unlocked something within her, had shown her what it was like to feel again and suddenly, nothing was the same anymore.

This had to stop, she upbraided herself.

She'd never been some moonstruck, feeble-minded female before. She knew better. She was tough and strong and didn't need anyone, least of all a man, to make her life meaningful. She did that all by herself.

By herself.

Alone.

The word taunted her. She was always alone, even in a crowd. Even when she was the center of it, the way she had been that last time when she had brought in that rapist who had jumped bail in Denver.

Max had made her feel as if she wasn't alone, as if she...

Stop it, she ordered. You'll make yourself crazy.

Maybe it was already too late for that.

"We'll be there soon," he was saying to her, his voice breaking through the clouds that were swirling around her brain.

She looked out the window. They were passing through endless sky and had been for hours. There wasn't even a single cloud formation to break up the monotony. She felt completely disoriented. "How can you tell?"

He tapped his wristwatch. "Because we've been in the air for a little over eight hours and I know how long it takes to reach the capital of Montebello."

She nodded carelessly, suddenly wishing that this was behind her and she could go on with her life.

Hoping that somehow, time could stand still long enough for her to harvest these moments.

And wasn't that crazy?

Maybe what she really needed, she decided, was to get away. To go somewhere on a vacation. A nice long vacation to recharge, reenergize and hopefully get her head together.

"Why don't you just sit back and enjoy the plane ride?" he suggested. Max called over the flight attendant and asked for a little light white wine for both of them.

"Trying to get me drunk?"

"As I recall," he thought back to the bar where she had drugged him, "it would probably take a dozen glasses to do that. I just want you to unwind a little before your spring pops out of its casing."

It was an odd thing to say, but she understood. And then, just before the wine arrived, Max placed his hand over hers and squeezed it.

Cara stopped wrestling with her thoughts.

The plane touched down at the airfield right on schedule. As Cara got out behind Max, she could see an extra-long black stretch limousine waiting for them. It reminded her of a panther that only gave the appearance of dozing in the hot sun. At any second, it could rev up and come alive.

Behind them, Weber was being hustled down the ramp, a guard at each elbow, his hands handcuffed behind him. A wealth of curses littered the air. Once on the ground, he was taken to another car, a far more functional, smaller one, and quickly whisked away to what she assumed was prison.

Who the hell was this man, she couldn't help wondering again. The king of a country didn't go through all this trouble just for a common American bail jumper, even one who, she was beginning to think, probably had an extensive rap sheet under several aliases.

"Please, come this way," a tall, elderly man with impeccable posture instructed.

"Hello, Albert, how are you?" Max asked, recognizing his uncle's personal secretary. He introduced Cara, who looked bemused.

"Very well, sir. It's a pleasure to see you here again, and with such a lovely companion." His expression never changed. "The king is looking forward to seeing you." Placing himself directly behind them, he escorted them to the waiting vehicle.

Getting in, Max was surprised to see that his uncle had come in person to meet them at the airstrip.

Even wearing a black blazer and gray slacks, he couldn't be mistaken for an ordinary man. In his late sixties, with a thick mane of almost white hair and dark eyes, Marcus Sebastiani was still very much a handsome man. His aristocratic bearing made it abundantly clear to anyone within ten yards of the man that they were in the presence of royalty.

Max made himself comfortable in the seat that faced his uncle, leaving plenty of room at his side for Cara. "Uncle Marcus, I didn't expect you to be here."

"What, and miss the chance of greeting my favorite nephew after all this time?" He smiled warmly at Max, leaning forward and gripping his hand in a firm handshake. "Not likely. We missed you at the wedding," he confided, referring to marriage of his daughter to the sheik's son. He didn't pause for a comment from Max.

"By the way," he winked, "don't tell your brother

about that favorite nephew business. After all, he is my godson and it would only dishearten him.'' His eyes alighted on Cara. There was approval in them almost instantly. ''And who have you brought me?''

Max nodded toward the airstrip. ''The guards just took—''

''No, not the prisoner,'' Marcus clarified. ''Who is this lovely creature?'' His eyes were warm as he took Cara's hand in his.

Max knew that, unlike his father, Marcus had a genuine affection for people, all people. His manner was not intended to disarm women he wanted to use for his own purposes.

Max's voice became more formal. ''King Marcus, may I present Ms. Cara Rivers.''

''Charmed, Ms. Rivers.'' His eyes holding hers, Marcus brought her hand to his lips and kissed it. As he lowered her hand, he still maintained a light hold, as if to form a link. ''And how is it that you are traveling with my nephew?''

The man was charming, but she was certain that his antennae had gone up. Off the top of her head, she guessed that the king was probably afraid she was some kind of gold digger.

''The duke and I share a common interest,'' she told him. ''Weber.''

Her answer couldn't have surprised Marcus more. He glanced at Max for an explanation. ''I don't think I understand. Are you somehow involved with that man?''

The king knew, by the very hue of her skin, that the young woman couldn't be related to Salim. And Marcus couldn't see the two of them together. The young woman before him looked too sharp to be taken in by the terrorist.

"Very much so," Cara responded. Out of the corner of her eye, she saw a look of amusement on Max's face. She pressed on. "He's my bounty."

This time Marcus really did look to Max for help. "I beg your pardon, I am not up on the latest American expressions."

"It's not an expression," Max told him. "It's a condition. There's a bounty out for Weber. He was involved in a burglary out on a ranch in Colorado. He fled the state after someone posted his bail. The bondsman needed to have him brought in before the trial date."

The king looked back to Cara. It was hard to believe she could be involved with something like that. "Which was?"

"Today," Cara told him.

"Oh, then we have cost you money." There was regret in the king's voice. "Allow me to—"

Generosity—or guilt—seemed to be a family trait, she thought. There were worse ones to have. "Thank you, Your Highness, but your nephew has already paid me for what would have been my loss."

"Oh. I see." He felt a surge of pride when he looked at Max. The young man was honorable, as always. As, apparently, was she. Otherwise, Marcus had no doubt that she would have attempted to extract money from him as well. He had known many women like that, women who had flocked to his late brother. "She is an honorable woman, Max. A rare find." His dark eyes shifted back to Cara. "So, am I to take it that you are—"

"A bounty hunter," she concluded for him, not sure if he was familiar with the term.

"A bounty hunter," Marcus repeated, shaking his head. He liked to think of himself as a progressive man, but this seemed to be beyond the pale. "Is this profession a wise choice for a young woman?"

"It is if she wants to eat and has limited avenues open to her. Besides—" Cara smiled at the king "—we can only follow our talents, Your Highness."

Tickled by the fire in spirit, Marcus laughed. "And yours is tracking men."

"Dangerous men," she qualified.

His eyes shifted to Max. The smile was slow, understanding.

"I see." He made up his mind about her. When it came to people, he never deliberated too long. "Will you do me the honor, Ms. Rivers, of joining us for dinner? I am holding a small dinner party in honor of Max's homecoming. Just a few friends, nothing formal."

She had a feeling that the king's idea of "nothing formal" was light years away from hers. "Which means what, leave my tiara in my room?"

Yes, Marcus definitely liked her spirit. She seemed like the right one for his often all-too-somber nephew. Someone to keep Max on his toes. The fact that she was beautiful only enhanced the match.

"Yes. Unless, of course, you wish to wear it." By his very intonation, he succeeded in making the conversation feel almost intimate. "I want you to be comfortable."

He might want it, but it wasn't going to happen, Cara thought. At bottom, she would always be the orphaned girl whose mother didn't want her. That sort of person hardly fit in with royalty.

But because she was a guest of the crown and it would be deemed impolite to refuse, Cara forced a smile into her eyes.

"I would love to join you for dinner, Your Highness."

Marcus clapped his hands together. There was nothing he liked more than a gathering of his closest, most trusted people, with a dash of fresh blood thrown in.

"Wonderful. Dinner is at seven. Max will come for you, won't you Max?"

"I'd have to," Max explained, in case she was going to say something about finding her own way around. "As I recall, there are a host of corridors and secret passageways in the palace, leaving a great many ways for a person to get lost."

"Even one who tracks dangerous men for a living," the king added with a wink.

The man could easily charm birds out of their tress, Cara thought. Not unlike his nephew.

Once they were at the palace and Cara was led off to her room, Max asked the king for a private audience. He wanted to talk about "Weber."

The king refused to even acknowledge that Max had asked a question at first. Instead he invited his nephew to come with him to see his garden. As interested in plant life and foliage as he was in translating the Dead Sea Scrolls, Max still found he had no choice but to follow his uncle and king.

In the center of the hedge configuration that he took

great pride in, Marcus turned to his nephew and abruptly said, "His name is not Kevin Weber, it is—"

"Jalil Salim, yes, I already know that." Surprised, pleased, his uncle raised a questioning brow for details. "I had my grandfather run 'Weber's' fingerprints through the international terrorist database. It kicked out Salim's name. The man has a staggering list of offenses." He could see why the King would want to see the man safely put away where he was no longer a threat to the Sebastianis and Montebello.

Marcus nodded. He'd been apprised that his nephew had looked Bill Ryker up when he had gone to live in California. "Ah yes, your grandfather. I only met him that one time, at your parents' wedding. He struck me as a fine man. To his credit, he raised a wonderful daughter all on his own." Max's grandmother had died when his mother was still a child. "How is he?"

"Alert, glad to be productive again."

Marcus knew more about the matter, knew that Max had started an investigative agency and had brought his grandfather in to work with him. "You gave him that."

Max saw it differently. His grandfather had taught him things he didn't know, had made patience a staple of his life. And given him a sense of family that had been missing when he had lived with his own father.

"We gave something to each other," Max corrected his uncle.

Marcus slipped his arm around his nephew's shoulder and laughed. Max was so unaffected, such a pleasure to be around. "Oh, Max, Max, Max, I have truly missed having you around."

"With all this intrigue surrounding the family, not to mention the palace, I doubt that you really have the time to notice that I'm gone."

Marcus sighed. Intrigue was the right word. "Oh, I notice all right. I notice. But let us not dwell on that for the moment. You have done well for yourself and I am glad of that." He paused, then slowly approached a subject he had a more personal interest in. "Tell me, am I wrong, or is there some sort of an electrical spark between you and the lady?"

"I'm not sure what there is between us."

"Mystery." Marcus nodded sagely, even though his eyes twinkled. "Always a good thing. There should always be mystery between a couple. It keeps them on their toes."

Max didn't trust his own feelings. They were all too new. "I think you're reading far too much into this, Uncle."

They differed there. "Haven't you heard? I am a great judge of people. And there is this look in your eyes I have never seen before…"

"Jet lag," Max interjected.

How typical of Max to shy away from this. How unlike his father the young man was. Though Antonio had been his own brother, Marcus had never approved of his womanizing ways, his cavalier treatment of Helen. A man took vows before God when he married, pledged his honor and his love. Those things could not taken lightly or shed because of a momentary hormonal reaction.

"I think not," the king contradicted. "But, I keep

you and you must be tired. Refresh yourself. Take a nap before dinner.''

Max saw that the king was beginning to walk back into the palace. ''We still haven't really talked.''

Marcus stopped only for a moment. ''You already know more than even Tyler told you. And we will talk. Later. I promise.'' Once more threading his arm around his nephew's shoulders, he ushered him toward the palace. ''For now, let me just enjoy having you back.''

Put that way, Max had no choice but to table his questions and follow his uncle's lead.

Nerves danced through Cara like tiny ice skaters with sharpened blades. It was like walking into a new foster home all over again. She could feel all eyes turning toward them.

Toward her.

''I feel like a fish out of water,'' Cara hissed in Max's ear as he escorted her into the dining room. It was beyond anything she could have ever imaged.

The dining room was the one his uncle used for intimate dinners comprised of only two dozen or so souls rather than the banquet hall, which was reserved for state dinners.

Max looked at the dress she was wearing. The one that had almost made him forget that the king was waiting for them. The one that had made him want to close the door behind him and skim his hands over her, rememorizing every curve that the long, slinky blue garment emphasized.

He lowered his head, bringing his lips close to her

ear. "Never saw a fish wearing anything like that, in or out of the water."

The comment could have been nothing more than a flippant remark, or a mildly polite observation. Why did a little thrill rush over her like that? He was a duke, accustomed to empty flattery. The words meant less than nothing.

They meant everything.

She'd found the dress laid out for her on the bed when she came out of a bathroom the size of a small movie theater. There had been no one around to ask about the garment's sudden appearance. It seemed to materialize out of nowhere.

Because she needed something to wear that wouldn't make Max ashamed of her.

As if that mattered, she told herself.

But it did.

It amazed her, when she tried it on, to discover that the dress was the right size. Wearing it, looking at herself in the mirror, she'd felt as if she was a little girl again. A little girl who still believed in magic.

Cara remembered how many times, as a child, she would pretend that someone was watching out for her. Someone who could magically supply whatever she needed whenever the need arose. It was just like having a fairy godmother.

There was, however, one thing wrong with the picture. As a child, she'd felt she belonged in such a setting. That it was her due.

As an adult, she knew differently.

She was out of her element here. Out of her depth. And with Max, she thought sadly, so out of her league it was painful.

So what was she doing here, playing the princess. Or duchess as it were?

She had no satisfactory answer.

Seeing them enter, the king smiled, broke protocol and rose in deference to the woman on Max's arm. Earlier she'd struck him as pretty. Now he realized he'd been wrong. She wasn't pretty. She was beautiful. And, it appeared, the perfect match for his nephew. He wondered what it would take for Max to realize that.

"Ah, you have found your way down here at last." He looked around at his other guests. "Everyone, Max has brought someone to our table. I'd like you all to meet Cara Rivers. From America."

There was a rush of voices, calling out greetings, saying her name. Cara's head spun as she tried to acknowledge everyone, focus on everyone.

Definitely out of her league, she thought.

Though she loved the silky feel of the long gown that she had on, she was far more at home in jeans and a button-down blouse. Far more at home behind the wheel of a car, tracking down a bail jumper or worse than attending a dinner party as fine as this. Max, on the other hand, she thought, looked as if he was born in that suit he was wearing.

To the manor born, she thought. It wasn't just a phrase, it was a truth.

"You're right, Marcus, she is lovely." A regal-looking woman sitting at the other end of the table smiled warmly at her.

This had to be Queen Gwendolyn, Cara thought. Unwilling to be taken for the consummate country bumpkin, Cara had used her time alone to quickly research the royal family via the internet.

A butler behind her pushed her chair in for her and Cara took her seat. A preponderance of utensils flanked her plate, daring her to pick the right one for the right course.

Oh God, she thought. She was better equipped to choose the right caliber gun to use than she was for this. Now what?

Chapter 15

Cara felt the press of Max's knee against hers. A warm shiver undulated through her that took effort to suppress.

Was he actually picking now to get friendly? Was it a turn-on for him to play sensual games at his uncle's table while his relatives sat, unsuspecting, around the perimeter?

Holding her breath, she waited for what she assumed was the next step: Max's hand to slip over her knee. Instead he moved his leg against hers a little more firmly. Confused, she glanced toward him.

His eyes indicated the silverware and then he picked up a small fork on the outer edge and began to eat his salad.

He wasn't playing hanky-panky, he was giving her silent table etiquette instructions.

The thought made her smile.

He was trying not to embarrass her. Either that, a small voice in her head whispered, or himself for bringing her.

No, she wasn't going to drive herself crazy with doubts now. She'd think about that later. Right now, she had a dinner to address and names to remember. With a slight inclination of her head in mute thanks, she picked up the correct fork just as the man who had been introduced to her as Max's brother, Duke Lorenzo, asked her a question.

"Very subtle of you," she murmured as the music enveloped them and she slipped one hand to Max's shoulder as he took the other and pressed it to his chest.

Dinner was over and the servants were clearing away the dishes. As coffee and after-dinner cordials were being served, it was time to really socialize. Assailed on both sides with people who were fascinated by what they'd discovered she did for a living, Cara found herself being rescued by Max, who asked her to dance.

Grateful for the breather and for an excuse to be in his arms, Cara rose from the table and allowed herself to be led off to the dance floor.

Holding Cara like this just made Max want to take her to his bed. He hardly felt like the same man anymore. All he could think about was her. Being with her, talking to her, inhaling the scent she always wore.

Making love with her.

He knew this had to stop, yet he felt powerless to do anything about it.

Which just made things worse.

For now, however, because protocol required he be here with her, he allowed himself to enjoy the moment and not wrestle with his thoughts or even think beyond the present.

"You're going to have to be more specific than that," he told her. Dancing past one of the queen's attendants, he nodded, acknowledging the latter's smile.

All Cara acknowledged was the woman's very shapely body and her very friendly smile toward Max.

"The silverware hints. Where I come from, we never had any more than two forks. One, usually." There hadn't always been that much to eat, either. Certainly not seven courses with side dishes arranged in an incredible array that teased the appetite and pleased the eye.

He thought of the tedious indoctrination process he and his brother had been forced through as children so that they wouldn't prove to be "an embarrassment to the house of Sebastiani."

"I always found a legion of forks and spoons a nuisance to keep track of." He smiled, remembering. "My mother always said that as long as you don't lower your head and eat off your plate like a starving vulture, you were ahead of the game."

Cara laughed, unmindful of the fact that her warm breath skimmed his face or that it aroused him. "Sounds like I would have liked your mother."

He found himself wishing that the two could have met. He had a feeling that Helen Sebastiani would have liked this unorthodox bounty hunter fate had led him to stumble across.

"Everyone did," he told her. "With the exception of my father."

She didn't waste time with polite protests that he was probably mistaken, the way some of his far more sophisticated guests might have. She'd seen the underbelly of life and knew a great deal about unhappiness. Life was too short for wasted breath. "Why did he marry her?"

The reason was as superficial as Max later found his father to be. "Because she was thought to be one of the most beautiful women in the world in her day. My mother was a beauty queen and then a top model. Her face was on every major magazine cover in the world and he claimed to have fallen in love with it."

How like his father to fall for a two-dimensional image, never taking the woman beneath into account. That was far too troublesome for Duke Antonio, too disturbing. That would have required, Max thought with some bitterness, a heart.

"He swept her away like a fairy-tale prince—or like a duke, as the case was." Max's jaw became rigid. "Once my father conquered something, he lost interest, went on to more exciting pursuits. It was no different when it came to my mother."

How sad, Cara thought. No happy endings in this fairy tale. "Why did your mother remain, then?"

Life was so modern now, people tended to forget what things were like even a mere twenty-five years ago.

"It's not so easy to get a divorce when a good portion of the world is watching you. Besides, my mother believed in marrying forever." Max danced Cara passed his uncle. The king, dancing with his wife, smiled broadly at them in approval. "And she had two children she knew she would never be allowed to take with her. Two children she would never abandon. She said that my father loved us, but he never spent any time with us. She wanted us to grow up feeling loved. So she stayed and threw herself into charity work to ease the pain."

Helen Sebastiani sounded like a wonderful woman. "Did it?"

The tempo slowed and so did he. Desire moved through him like an ever swelling army.

"She never complained. But I suspect it didn't. There was a pain in her eyes she couldn't mask." He looked down at Cara. He'd said far more than he'd intended, finding her easy to talk to. Talking wasn't a luxury he usually allowed himself. "Why are you asking all these questions about my family?"

For once, the look she gave him was completely devoid of guile.

"Because I have no family of my own to talk about." And then the reason that was probably behind his question hit her. "Don't worry." She winked. "This isn't being reprinted in the Trashy Tabloid of the Week."

Her wink went straight to his gut, wreaking havoc. His hand tightened around hers.

"Old news anyway." He forced himself to loosen his fingers from about hers. "You look exceptionally beautiful tonight."

"But?" Cara waited for the inevitable qualification, hoping it wouldn't sting too badly.

"No 'but.'" Try as he might, he didn't quite understand her. "Why do you always expect something bad to follow something good?"

"Because it usually does," she said simply. "And I like being prepared."

The orchestra began playing another song, its rhythm slightly faster than the last. He ignored the increased tempo. He liked swaying gently with her. It suited his mood. "Maybe it would do you more good to expect something good."

Cara shrugged, looking away for a moment. "Those kinds of surprises I don't need to be prepared for. I can handle them just fine."

But avoiding eye contact was for cowards and she had vowed a long time ago never to be a coward again. Instead she changed the topic to something safer and less close to her heart, which was in jeopardy of being breached.

"So, any news?" she asked, changing the topic. "When can I take our mutual creep back to Colorado with me?"

He'd been hoping that wouldn't come up tonight. Max didn't want to talk shop, didn't want anything to spoil the evening. An evening that he was hoping would end in her room.

But since she'd asked, he couldn't lie to her. "I'm afraid that it's going to be awhile."

Her pace slowed until she stopped dancing entirely. "Oh? And why is that?"

His hand still wrapped around hers, he forced her to move to the tempo he set. He didn't want any attention drawn to the argument he suddenly saw brewing.

"Because his list of offenses here is far more extensive than the one in the U.S. Salim is thought to be responsible for several bombing raids and the king thinks he might have had a hand in bringing down the prince's plane.''

She vaguely remembered hearing the story about a year ago. Something about a prince's plane crashing in the Rockies. The name of the country hadn't registered until now.

She looked at him in surprise. ''That was your prince?''

''More than that,'' Max clarified. ''That was my cousin.''

The news stunned her into silence for a moment. His cousin. She wondered if they'd been close and if this was all really a personal matter. She could feel sympathy rising inside her, but quickly banked it down. She couldn't afford that, not now. There was too much at stake. She had given her word to the sheriff as well as making a promise to Phil, who was technically out a large amount of money until things got squared away in a court regarding the extradition.

''Look, I'm very sorry about your cousin, I really am, but still, I can't—''

Max couldn't quite read her tone, but there was an edgy look in her eyes. As if she was waiting for a trap to snap, or to be pushed out of a plane without benefit of a parachute.

''There's no need to be upset. I've already covered the bounty money,'' he reminded her.

She could feel her hackles going up. Did he think he could just buy her off like some strolling hostess of the evening that had given him a good time? She'd thought he'd understood her better than that. Obviously she was giving him too much credit.

It figured. "It's not just about the bounty money."

What was she getting so annoyed about? "You said the other day that it was. That you didn't care what the sheriff and I did with the prisoner as long as you got the bounty money. I believe dancing was mentioned," he said in an effort to get her to smile and drop the subject.

So now was he laughing at her? He was certainly making her sound callous and greedy. Was that what he thought of her? Was she just someone to buy off?

Well, why shouldn't he think of her that way? Look at the world she came from. Look at where he came from. The mountains and flatlands, that's what they were. And the mountains looked down at the flatlands.

She gritted her teeth together, enunciating every word. "It's about giving my word to the sheriff that I'd bring Weber back."

"It's Salim," he reminded her. "Jalil Salim, not Kevin Weber. And as I remember, your word was rather twistable."

Incensed, she pulled her hand away from his. "Not to the people who count."

He read between the lines and her tone. "And I don't count."

Cara's chin shot up. "Now who's twisting things around?"

The woman blew hot and cold at the same time. He was getting very weary of this dance of words. "You tell me."

Right, big joke. Cara's eyes narrowed, pinning him.

"I don't think anyone can tell you anything. You seem to have the answers to everything." Afraid that she was going to say something that might offend the people around her, she gathered up her skirt, preparing to go. "If you'll excuse me, I think I've had enough old world charm for one evening."

There was a huge pain in the middle of her chest that was working its way up her throat and seriously campaigning against her eyes. She could feel tears forming. Alarmed, she began to plow her way off the dance floor, brushing passed Lorenzo.

"Is something wrong?" the duke asked.

She stopped only long enough to be polite. "I suddenly have a splitting headache. If you'll excuse me, I need to lie down."

Lorenzo turned toward his older brother, glad that Max had finally found someone. "Looks like you have a regular spitfire on your hands."

As far as Max was concerned, the old-fashioned term described Cara Rivers to a *t*. She was spitting fire all right.

And he felt fire burning through him every time he took her into his arms.

"Not at the moment," he corrected his younger brother, indicating his empty hands. "But I—"

The king came up behind him, placing a hand on his shoulder. "Max, would you mind giving me a moment? I'd like you to take a walk with me in the garden."

Max hesitated, torn. He wanted to go after Cara, to smooth over whatever it was that had gotten wrinkled. But maybe it would do her some good to have a few minutes to herself. To get whatever bur had gotten under her blanket out and become civilized again.

He turned toward his uncle and inclined his head. "Of course."

Max gestured for the king to lead the way.

"I know you're here for only a short while, Max, but I have to confess I have always valued having you as my sounding board." They were in the garden now, away from the lights of the palace and from prying ears. The king relaxed, looking at his nephew fondly. "You, above anyone, have always demonstrated that you have no ulterior motives when it comes to the affairs of this country, no dark side behind your opinions."

His uncle looked so serious. Max pushed aside his own concerns, placing himself completely at his uncle's disposal. "What's on your mind?"

"As you know, we believe now that Lucas survived the plane crash. The fact that he is most likely alive is being kept a secret from everyone except those who are closest to me. When I initially renewed my search for Lucas, very few people were informed." Agitation caused him to pace as he spoke. "Only those within the family and what I believed were a trusted few members of Sheik Ahmed's family knew." His expression grew grim as he thought of the information his agents had brought him. "We have confirmed that Salim knew we were searching for Lucas, that we had new evidence that he was alive." Marcus looked at his nephew. "I have received news that Salim's mission was not only to set up a front for the Brothers of Darkness in America, but to track down my son and to kill him."

The king drew a deep breath, the very thought wounding his heart. "How could he, a member of the Brothers of Darkness, have known any of this unless someone from the Kamal family told him?" To believe it was someone within his own family was unthinkable and he refused to even remotely entertain the idea. That only left his new son-in-law's family.

The new peace was fragile. He had to tread carefully. If he was wrong...

Max was piecing things together as quickly as they were being thrown at him. "Then you suspect—"

Marcus waved one hand helplessly in the air. "I don't know who to suspect."

The king sighed, hating the intrigue which had once seemed to spark his adolescent heart. Now he longed for only peace. Peace that insisted on eluding him.

"I have asked Gage Weston—another duke who refuses to assume his title," he interjected with a smile as he looked at Max, "to investigate this matter for me. To that end he will be attempting to work his way into the Kamals's trust."

Max was still unclear on why the revelation was being made to him at this time. "And you are sharing this with me because?"

The king smiled, knowing he could be both blunt and honest with his nephew the way he couldn't with others. "Because I want you to tell me if you think I am seeing boogie men where there are only harmless shadows in the night."

When it came to the family members he cared about, Max felt that it never hurt for them to be too cautious. "We both know that the Brothers of Darkness are a force to be reckoned with and to be wary of. No, I don't think you're being unduly cautious." For his uncle's sake, he bent the truth a little. "In your position, I would do exactly the same thing."

But Marcus knew him too well. "No, in my position, you would have tried to find things out on your own, gone into the heart of the clan and taken it on, one member at a time," Marcus pointed out. "Because, at your age, I would have toyed with the same thought. However, with age comes wisdom—and slowness. I cannot say which it is that is the deciding factor."

Max smiled at the man he had often wished fate had made his father instead of his uncle. "You will never grow old, Uncle, only wiser."

Marcus laughed heartily. "I knew there was a reason you were always my favorite." He slipped his arm around the other man's shoulders. "Come, we have kept your young woman waiting long enough. I saw the way your brother was looking at her."

Max knew that it was just harmless teasing on his uncle's part. The friendly rivalry that had existed between them as boys had never extended to the women in their lives. It was as if, without saying a word about it, out of a respect for their mother, both of them were trying not to emulate their father's life.

"She's not waiting, she's gone."

"Gone?" Marcus stopped walking. "Gone where?"

Max upbraided himself silently. He hadn't meant

it to sound as melodramatic as that. "To her room, probably. To cool off."

Relieved, Marcus shook his head, doling out friendly advice. "Oh, I don't think you would want that one too cool, Max. She reminds me of someone who would warm your heart for many decades to come."

Max thought of the look on Cara's face just before she'd spun on her heel and stormed away. And if ever a woman had stormed, it was Cara Rivers. "I don't think she sees things in that light."

They'd had a tiff, an argument, Marcus thought. Good. What was affection without adversity? Bland.

"You were always a negotiator, Max. Negotiate. Unless you have no feelings for her." Marcus pretended to peer into his eyes. "But you do."

Max didn't like having his thoughts invaded this way, even by a beloved uncle. Especially when he didn't feel as if he had sorted any of this out himself.

"I don't know."

"I do. You have your father's eyes."

Marcus stiffened just a little. "I'd rather you didn't compare me to him."

Marcus understood perfectly. They were alike in their regard for Antonio. Death had allowed them to commiserate. "Your father had magnificent eyes. It was the condition of his soul we questioned." Marcus touched Max's face fondly. "You have your mother's soul. Beautiful, sensitive and enormous." He patted Max's shoulder and then gave him a little push. "Go to her, Max, make things right. For both of you."

Max shrugged. He didn't want to rush things. "Maybe in a little while."

"The stubbornness you exhibit is your grandfather's," Marcus told him. "Have it your way. But don't let too much time pass."

Slipping an arm around the younger man's shoulder again, the king turned back toward the palace.

Cara moved around the luxurious room like someone confined to a prison cell.

There was no point in her remaining.

If the king had no intention of releasing Weber-Salim, or whoever the creep was, to her any time soon, she couldn't just hang around here like some bump on a log, waiting indefinitely.

Maybe Max could afford to do nothing with his time, but she couldn't. She had a living to make. The ten thousand dollars would tide Bridgette over for just so long. And they both knew that Bridgette's health was not what it used to be. Cara wanted to be prepared to help if Bridgette needed it.

Besides, staying here was awkward and just plain painful. Everywhere she looked reminded her of how different she and Max really were.

She looked in the mirror, seeing the dress that had been left for her. As if whoever left it already had known that she couldn't have packed anything remotely suitable for this evening. No one asked. It was a given.

There wasn't a future for them.

Hell, there wasn't even a present. She'd seen the way some of the other women had looked at Max during dinner. As if he was a prize that they meant to win. She couldn't compete against women like that and she wasn't about to lower herself by trying.

She'd had enough humiliation in her life, she didn't need any more.

It was nice while it lasted, she thought, but all fairy tales ended. And if she remembered her Hans Christian Anderson, they didn't all end with "And they lived happily ever after." Some didn't live happily at all.

That would be her, she thought.

But she had her pride and, no matter what Max seemed to think to the contrary, her honor. She was leaving with those intact. If she stayed, it might turn out to be another story.

Cara abruptly stopped pacing before her closet. The maid had already hung everything up and placed the suitcase in the recesses. Cara pulled it out. What she needed to do was to get her things together and leave before Max knew anything about her plans to go.

They had to have some flight leaving here for the States, didn't they? The airport wasn't far from the palace. She could just have someone drive her to the airport and take it from there.

It was a viable plan.

Her head jerked around as she heard a noise on the terrace.

Ryker.

Her heart began to hammer. Had he snuck onto her terrace to try to get her to go back to the party? Maybe it had been rude of her to leave that way, she thought, guilt nibbling at her conscience. After all, it wasn't the king's fault that she'd fallen in love with Max.

The thought jarred her down to her toes.

Love?

When had that happened?

No, it wasn't love, she insisted silently, it was lust, pure—or not so pure—and simple. Well, maybe not simple, either, but—

Damn, what had he done to her? Her brain felt like Swiss cheese.

She threw open the terrace door to confront Max and perhaps her own wavering thoughts.

"Look, don't come skulking around here. I'm not going to—"

Her words vanished as Salim grabbed her by the throat and shoved her back into her room.

Chapter 16

By the time Max and his uncle had returned from the garden to the dining area, Max had decided to call it an early evening.

There was a knowing look in the king's eyes as he looked at him.

"I understand. There are things you have to tend to." There was a wistful smile on his face. "Tread careful, Max. Be sure things aren't said in haste that you'll regret later."

"I'll do my best," Max promised. Although with Cara, that wasn't always possible, he added silently.

About to leave, Max's attention was drawn to the guard who came hurrying into the room. Seeking out the king, he whispered something in his monarch's ear.

Marcus's expression changed immediately.

Gone was the smile, replaced with the look of a

leader who had once given serious thought to making a career within his country's military.

"Are you certain?" he asked the guard, his voice deadly calm.

"Yes, Your Highness. One dead, three wounded. But only he escaped."

At his uncle's elbow, Max had an uneasy feeling. "What's wrong?"

Marcus turned to him, his olive complexion uncharacteristically pale. "Salim has escaped. Someone killed the main guard at the prison. They think the escape was engineered by a person or persons associated with the Brothers of Darkness."

It didn't matter who had engineered it, what mattered now was that Jalil Salim was free. And that he'd sworn vengeance against him and more importantly, against Cara.

A sense of panic Max had never experienced before suddenly took root.

He had to get to her before Salim did.

"Your Highness," the guard was saying, "one of the guards said just before he lost consciousness he saw Salim and his men fleeing to the hills. Salim might be miles from here by now."

The king was too aware of the fact that nothing was ever what it seemed. "And then again, he might not. Where is this guard now?" Marcus wanted to know.

"They were taking him to the hospital as I left."

"Send someone there, then and find out as much as you can." Marcus ordered. "And get as many men as you can together. Salim is not going to escape us a second time." Turning, he started to say something to Max, only to see that his nephew was hurrying away. "Do you know where to find him?"

"I'm hoping I don't," Max tossed over his shoulder. He didn't have time to stay and elaborate. Not if what he was most afraid of was true.

Afraid. He had never been afraid for himself. Not even as a child and never as a solider. That was what had made him so good at what he did. He was cautious only insofar as he did not want to alert his quarry, but fear for his own well being never held him in check, never held him back.

He was afraid now. Very afraid.

But again, not for himself.

Adrenaline shot through Cara with both barrels as she found herself staring into the dark eyes of a madman. Salim was cutting the air off from her windpipe, choking her. Clawing at his hand, Cara dug her nails into his flesh and raked them down.

Yelping, Salim let her go, only to grab her arm as she tried to get away. He slammed her against the wall viciously.

She hit the back of her head. The room started to spin as she tried vainly to focus on something, to keep it fixed in place.

"What—what are you doing here?" she managed to spit out.

Even before he answered, she knew. He was going to kill her.

"Keeping my promise," Salim snarled, his unshaven face inches from hers. "I said I would kill you and that lowly scum you were with and now I will."

Her blood turned to ice in her veins. There was no doubt in her mind that this man could kill a hundred people and not feel anything but a sense of satisfaction.

Killing her would be easy.

The hell it will, she silently promised. She was not going to go out that easily.

There was no terror in her eyes. Salim wanted terror. "Beg for your life, you miserable bitch."

She wouldn't give him the satisfaction. Instead she glared at Salim defiantly, knowing that in the end begging would do no good, it would only feed something depraved inside him.

"No."

Enraged, he twisted her arm so hard, Cara sank down on her knees before him, unable to stand.

"Beg," he roared maniacally.

Dizzy, with pain shooting through her arm, she sank her teeth into his thigh.

Screaming, Salim let her go, staggering backward.

As she scrambled to her feet to get away, Salim grabbed a fistful of her hair and yanked her back. The guttural cry that escaped her lips was completely involuntary.

Running down the corridor, Max heard the cry.

He didn't remember taking the last several yards to her door, hardly remembered hurling himself against the dark mahogany barrier. Horrible scenarios were all crowding his brain at once, chilling his heart as he broke into the room.

Still holding her by her hair, Salim pulled Cara to her feet. A gun appeared from nowhere in his hand. He aimed it straight at Max.

Max curbed his impulse to hurl himself at the man. Salim was crazy, he could turn the gun on Cara instead and shoot her. "There's no way you'll get out of the palace alive."

Salim narrowed his eyes malevolently. Feeble-minded infidel, didn't he understand that all this was for a greater good, a higher power? Lives, even his, were unimportant.

"Perhaps, perhaps not. But this I promise you— the two of you will be dead by then. You and this worthless bitch."

As his lips peeled back in a satisfied grin, Salim cocked his weapon, keeping the gun barrel trained straight at Max's head.

"No," Cara shrieked, throwing her weight against Salim's hip as she simultaneously grabbed his arm to throw his aim off.

Pain seared through her scalp as she could feel her hair being pulled out. The pain radiated all through her, down to her arm and her chest. Something felt as if it had burst into her shoulder.

Her vision blurred again as she saw Max leap over a table and throw himself at Salim. The gun had fallen to the floor.

So had she, Cara realized. Crawling over to the weapon, fighting an almost paralyzing feeling with fire streaming all through her, she managed to grab the gun and struggle to her knees.

The two men in the room were locked in mortal combat. Salim was behind Max. His powerful arm locked around Max's neck, the terrorist was choking him.

"Let him go!" she ordered Salim.

Suddenly Max sank down to one knee and threw the man over his head. Salim crashed to the floor just as the king's personal guard came rushing into the room. The king was right behind them.

"Take him," Marcus ordered angrily. "And this time, see that you keep him. I don't want anything to happen to him until he talks to me." After that, he added silently, the man's fate was in the hands of God and the guards.

Dragging air into his depleted lungs, Max had turned to Cara.

Feeling weaker by the moment, she let the weapon fall from her hands.

"Are you all right?" she asked him.

Wobbly, Cara tried to rise to her feet, but her knees didn't seem to want to work.

"Oh God, you're bleeding." There was blood all over her gown, blocking the source of the wound. Real fear bit into him with numerous, sharp, pointy teeth. Max quickly picked her up into his arms before she could fall the rest of the way to the floor. "The bastard shot you."

"All in a day's work," she managed to mumble before her head fell back and the world, and Max and the room melted away.

The sensation of motion surrounding her penetrated Cara's fuzzy brain a second before she came to moments later.

Her eyes were almost too heavy to open, but with superhuman effort she managed to push the lids up.

Max was rushing down the long hallway with her.

There was someone with him, a man she thought, but she couldn't be sure.

"What...?"

Thank God she was conscious. He was afraid she'd lapsed into a coma.

"Don't try to talk," Max cautioned. "We're taking you to the hospital."

"I don't need a hospital," she protested. She tried to get struggle of his arms. Or thought she tried. But there was no strength to draw on. Her arms felt absolutely useless. Both of them.

The woman brought new meaning to the word stubborn. Max took it as a good sign.

"You've been shot and you fainted, you need a doctor," he told her firmly.

His voice echoed in Cara's head, as if they were both standing in some kind of cave. But it was too bright for a cave. Caves weren't bright, were they?

"I didn't faint," she protested, using up all her available breath for the few words.

Beyond stubborn, Max thought, angrily. But alive. Thank God, alive.

"All right," he allowed, "you took a short nap. But you're still going to the hospital." Outside now, he looked around. Someone behind him said, "Over there," pointing to the limousine. Max rushed over to the king's car. "I'm not about to lose you just because you're too pigheaded to admit you need help."

"You...can...help if...you...want," she breathed, each word an effort. "But I don't...need...it."

In the back seat of the limousine, Max sat, holding her on his lap, his arms wrapped around her as he cradled her against him.

He'd just said something to her. What was it? Her brain was having trouble holding onto things. Something about losing her.

Was he trying to lose her?

Or was he...

Nothing made any sense so she stopped trying to make it. All she was aware of was the pain licking its way through her body and the strong arms that were around her. Trying to keep her safe.

Sighing, she curled into him.

"See, I told you. It's just a flesh wound." Cara shifted impatiently on the gurney, wanting to get going already.

"A deep flesh wound," he reminded her of the doctor's diagnosis.

Forced into a hospital gown, Cara reached down for the dress that had gotten ruined. She looked at it a little remorsefully.

"A deep flesh wound," she echoed indulgently. "Nothing that won't heal." She pressed her lips together, trying to organize chaotic thoughts that refused to hold still for the process. She hated admitting this, but she hated not knowing more. "I'm a little fuzzy, did we get him?"

"Yes, and this time, he's being kept under heavy guard. There won't be any repeat performances of tonight, I promise you." He'd almost lost her tonight. Max found the thought unbearable.

"Good." She began to nod her head and thought better of it. Even the slightest movement seemed to echo in her brain. "Because I'm not sure how much more blood I have left to give to this cause." She didn't feel like moving. Cara looked at him. "I guess you saved my life."

He inclined his head and then smiled. He didn't want to think about what would have happened if he'd been just a little slower.

"And you saved mine."

She blew out a breath. "They cancel each other out, then."

He knew what she was doing and he wasn't going to let her get away with it that easily. "Not quite. In the Chinese culture, a life you save is yours forever."

He was stretching things. "But you're not Chinese and neither am I."

Max shook his head, refusing to let her shrug this off. "Doesn't matter."

Okay, she'd play along. "I guess that means that your life's mine."

He resisted the temptation of drawing her to him. Not yet. "And yours belongs to me."

There was one logical approach to this, she thought. "Trade you."

He laughed. "I don't think so."

Cara pressed her lips together, afraid to let her mind go beyond the immediate moment. "So what are we going to do with these two lives we've got on our hands?"

He tread slowly, testing the waters. Not wanting to scare her away. "Perhaps it means that we'll have to spend them together. I wouldn't want to see you misusing 'my' life."

Her face was starting to lose its pale pallor. A twinkle entered her eyes. "Or you mine. Exactly what is it that you had in mind?"

"A partnership." He watched her face as he spoke, wrapping his fingers around a small paper band in his pocket. "I've got more cases at my agency than I can handle and I could use a good investigator on the staff."

He was offering her work. This was about work. Well, all right, she thought, making the best of it, trying to ignore the very real pang she felt because for a second, she'd thought, hoped, it was about something more. She was due for a change and she'd bet that his line of work paid better than hers.

"Not staff," she reminded him. "Partner."

Max nodded, knowing that she'd catch him on this. "Right."

She blew out another breath, still struggling to steady her bearings. Her shoulder where the bullet had been dug out was beginning to throb. The medicine was wearing off. She knew it would get worse. "So we'll be working together."

He could hardly contain himself, but because of the ground he was covering, he had to. "Yes."

Her eyes looked into his. What would she have done if that dirtbag would have killed Max? She didn't think she could have borne it. "And living together?"

His baby steps had decreased into half that. "Is that what you want?"

She huffed. She'd been shot, and he was trying to play games with her? "I'm asking you what *you* want."

Cara felt like punching him for the grin that curved his mouth. He was laughing at her, having fun at her expense. Maybe he didn't even mean that bit about being partners.

"I thought you were a liberated woman who did whatever she wanted."

"Yes, I am." Her patience, never at a premium, was beginning to disintegrate. "And what this liberated woman wants is to hear what's on your mind."

The smile remained, but his eyes grew serious. "How about what's in my heart?"

She realized she'd stopped breathing and took in a deep breath. "I'm flexible, you can start with another part of your anatomy."

He cupped her face gently. "Cara—"

Her pulse began to go into double time again. "Oh-oh, it's getting personal."

He didn't want to dance this strange, guarded dance any longer. "It has to get personal. I'm not about to say I love you to a stranger."

Her eyes widened at the revolution that came out of nowhere. "You love me?"

"Yes." He didn't see why he had to spell it out for her. "Haven't you figured that out yet? I thought you were a good investigator."

"I am," she protested, "but I never claimed to be a mind reader."

"Then read this." Taking her hand, he opened it and placed her palm against his chest.

Her breath was growing short in her lungs again. She licked her lips nervously. "It's beating."

"For you."

And then she smiled. Really smiled.

He could have gotten lost in her smile, but he knew

that was probably her plan. To decoy him. "Don't you have something you have to say to me?"

"That's nice?" she offered innocently. When she saw the storm clouds gathering in his eyes, Cara became serious. Nerves rose up within her, colliding like butterflies that had had too much to drink. "All right, all right, this isn't easy for me. Every time I've gotten attached to someone, they've pulled away from me, given me back."

She was afraid, he realized. Maybe that made two of them. He took her into his arms. "I've already unwrapped you and taken your tags off, Cara. I can't give you back." His eyes caressed her face. "I don't *want* to give you back."

Oh God, he was going to make her cry. She hated to cry. "Then what do you want?"

Instead of answering her, he reached into his pocket and took out the small paper band. Taking her left hand in his, he slipped the band on her third finger.

She stared at it, afraid to pull her thoughts together. "What is this?"

"A cigar band. I got it from my uncle while the doctor was working on you." Maybe the wound had given her amnesia. "Like in that story you told Sheriff Adler's wife, remember?"

"I remember," she whispered, emotion choking off her voice.

"I want you to marry me, Cara."

More than anything, she wanted to believe that it was possible. But she was a realist and she knew that there was no place for the mountains and the flatlands to meet.

"And what, live here?" She looked away. "I don't fit in."

He raised her chin with his hand and forced her to look at him. "No, back in California. I already told you, I want you to work with me and that's where my agency is. And you fit in everywhere," he told her firmly. "You just have to give yourself permission to believe that."

There was a place where the mountains and the flatlands met. At the very junction. Maybe, just maybe, this could work. God knew she loved him enough to make it work. "You're serious."

He raised his hand as if he were taking an oath. "Every word."

She smiled, relaxing a little. "Then I guess it's safe to love you."

But Max shook his head. "It's never going to be safe," he told her. When she looked confused, he explained, "You thrive on excitement, remember?"

After tonight, she'd had enough excitement to last a very long time.

"Having you love me is exciting enough," Cara assured him.

He let go of the breath he'd been holding all along. "Then it's yes?"

If she were any happier, she thought, she'd probably light up like a beacon. "Yes. How can I resist the man who holds my life in the palm of his hand?"

There was only one thing left out, one thing to make this perfect. He looked into her eyes. "Tell me," he coaxed.

She knew what he wanted. The words hovered on her lips, refusing to come out. They'd been beaten back so many times, she could get over the last hurdle. "You already know."

Yes, he knew. He could see it in her eyes, feel it in the way she touched him. But that still didn't change things.

"I want to hear the words, Cara." He took her left hand in his. "You're not the only one who needs them."

Cara looked at him, suddenly becoming aware of something that hadn't occurred to her before. That perhaps this son of royalty needed love as much as she did.

Her heart swelled as she realized that after all these years, she had found her soul mate. And she'd only had to come halfway around the world to do it.

Slipping her one good arm around his neck, she looked up into his eyes. "I love you, Ryker."

"Max," he corrected. "It's always been Max."

"Yes," her smile lit up her eyes just before he brought his mouth down to hers, "it has."

*   *   *   *   *

ROMANCING THE CROWN

continues next month with

SECRET-AGENT SHEIK

by Linda Winstead Jones,
featuring royal son Sheik Hassan Kamal
as he fights to help the crown of
Montebello—and loses his heart to the
enemy's daughter.

Only from Silhouette Intimate Moments!
Here's a sneak preview....

Chapter One

Elena stood at the tall window in her office and glanced down into the parking lot. Sheik Hassan Kamal arrived right on time, whipping a black Ferrari into the parking lot two minutes before their meeting was set to begin. He took long, arrogant strides through the parking lot. His traditional costume—*gutra,* long jacket and baggy pants, all stark white—whipped around him as he made his way toward the building entrance with what could only be called impatience in his step.

Elena was not nervous about meeting Sheik Hassan, she had told herself all morning. She wanted to make a good impression because if this merger went through it could be important. Not so much for the company, which was stable financially, but for her father's home country, Maloun, and the sheik's country, Tamir. Relations were difficult and had been for a very long time. A unity of some sort with the royal family of Tamir might help to stabilize those relations.

Her father didn't think so. He had ordered her to show the sheik around, be polite, and then decline any offers of a partnership. She had hopes that she could change his mind before the sheik's visit was over.

She only hoped she could maintain her patience with the sheik. She had little use for men who lived their lives the way he did. No responsibilities. Too much money and not enough common sense. Sheik Hassan Kamal was nothing more than a large, spoiled child looking for a new plaything, and he'd set his sights on *her* refinery.

The elevator on her floor sounded with a ping as the door opened. Elena proceeded into the outer office to greet the sheik.

He stepped from the hallway into the office with the same arrogance that had carried him through the parking lot. For a moment Elena was literally speechless. Kamal was tall, a good six foot two, and broad in the shoulders. He looked bigger face-to-face than he had from her window view. She tried to tell herself it was the traditional costume that made him seem imposing. But she couldn't fool herself. This man was powerfully built. Strong and hard. The power that emanated from him had nothing to do with what he wore.

Even with sunglasses hiding his eyes from her, she could tell that he had an unusually handsome, olive-toned face. The cut of his jaw was sharp and masculine, the nose perfectly straight and fittingly regal, and the mouth…a mouth that sensuous should be illegal!

"Welcome to Rahman Oil," she said, recovering quickly and stepping forward, offering her hand for a crisp, businesslike handshake. The sheik took her hand in his, grasped it firmly, and brought it to his lips. She was so shocked when he touched her knuckles with that illegal mouth of his that she literally jumped. A tingle shimmied up her arm and to her neck, where it settled in. The sheik wore a small, completely wicked smile as he returned to an upright position and gradually released her hand, very lightly trailing his fingers over her palm.

"If I had known that Mr. Rahman had such an enchanting secretary, I would have arrived early so I could spend time with you before my meeting. Perhaps he will be kind enough to leave me waiting for a few minutes." His English was almost perfect, his voice deep and sweet as honey.

"Secretary?" Elena said with a smile of her own. "Mr. Kamal, I'm…"

"Hassan," he interrupted. "Such an enchanting lady must call me by my given name. And yours is…"

"Elena," she answered, wondering how long it would take Kamal to realize his mistake.

"A beautiful name," he said, removing his sunglasses and giving Elena her first good, full look at his face. The eyes were black, deep and penetrating and as sensuous as his mouth.

"Elena Rahman," she said.

His smile widened. "Then you are also a relation

of the owner, Yusef Rahman? How nice to find that this is a true family business.''

''Elena Jumanah Rahman.''

It took a moment, but his smile eventually faded. ''E.J. Rahman,'' he said slowly.

''Exactly.'' Elena was accustomed to the old-world attitudes of her father and his friends. If Yusef Rahman had fathered a son, she would not be in this position. She would not be CEO, and she would not have a degree in chemical engineering. But there was no son, there was only Elena, to Yusef Rahman's life-long dismay.

She found Kamal's disconcerted expression rather amusing. He had obviously not planned to do business with a woman. ''Would you like to step into my office?''

Hassan sat facing Elena Rahman. They were separated by a desk, two cups of terrible, weak coffee, and several unorganized piles of paperwork. He was still astounded that Rahman Oil's CEO was a woman! And an amazingly beautiful one, at that. Such a woman should have better, more appropriate pursuits to fill her time. He could think of a few, sitting here watching her as she told him all about Rahman Oil and the operations of their refinery.

She did seem to be knowledgeable, he would give her that. They had been discussing the refinery for over an hour, and she had answered every one of his questions without referring to notes or calling on an assistant. The CEO of Rahman Oil was not a mere figurehead. She knew what she was doing.

Hassan focused his thoughts. He was here on a mission, to discover whether the refinery was the head-quarters for the terrorist group called the Brothers of Darkness. Not to romance a woman, no matter how tempting.

Surely Elena Rahman was not involved with the Brothers of Darkness. Not only was it unlikely that the Brothers would allow a woman into their organization, he was certain that he saw honesty and sincerity in Elena's green eyes. She was open, direct and earnest, and she had no qualms about looking him squarely in the eye. The longer he watched and listened to her, the more convinced he was of her integrity.

He set the certainty of her innocence aside. Appearances could be deceiving, and anything...anything was possible.

This Mother's Day Give Your Mom A Royal Treat

Win a fabulous one-week vacation in Puerto Rico for you and your mother at the luxurious Inter-Continental San Juan Resort & Casino. The prize includes round trip airfare for two, breakfast daily and a mother and daughter day of beauty at the beachfront hotel's spa.

INTER·CONTINENTAL

San Juan

RESORT & CASINO

Here's all you have to do:

Tell us in 100 words or less how your mother helped with the romance in your life. It may be a story about your engagement, wedding or those boyfriends when you were a teenager or any other romantic advice from your mother. The entry will be judged based on its originality, emotionally compelling nature and sincerity. See official rules on following page.

Send your entry to:

Mother's Day Contest

In Canada
P.O. Box 637
Fort Erie, Ontario
L2A 5X3

In U.S.A.
P.O. Box 9076
3010 Walden Ave.
Buffalo, NY
14269-9076

Or enter online at www.eHarlequin.com

All entries must be postmarked by April 1, 2002. Winner will be announced May 1, 2002. Contest open to Canadian and U.S. residents who are 18 years of age and older. No purchase necessary to enter. Void where prohibited.

PRROY

Two ways to enter:

• **Via The Internet:** Log on to the Harlequin romance website (www.eHarlequin.com) anytime beginning 12:01 a.m. E.S.T., January 1, 2002 through 11:59 p.m. E.S.T., April 1, 2002 and follow the directions displayed on-line to enter your name, address (including zip code), e-mail address and in 100 words or fewer, describe how your mother helped with the romance in your life.

• **Via Mail:** Handprint (or type) on an 8 1/2" x 11" plain piece of paper, your name, address (including zip code) and e-mail address (if you have one), and in 100 words or fewer, describe how your mother helped with the romance in your life. Mail your entry via first-class mail to: Harlequin Mother's Day Contest 2216, (in the U.S.) P.O. Box 9076, Buffalo, NY 14269-9076; (in Canada) P.O. Box 637, Fort Erie, Ontario, Canada L2A 5X3.

For eligibility, entries must be submitted either through a completed Internet transmission or postmarked no later than 11:59 p.m. E.S.T., April 1, 2002 (mail-in entries must be received by April 9, 2002). Limit one entry per person, household address and e-mail address. On-line and/or mailed entries received from persons residing in geographic areas in which entry is not permissible will be disqualified.

Entries will be judged by a panel of judges, consisting of members of the Harlequin editorial, marketing and public relations staff using the following criteria:
  • Originality - 50%
  • Emotional Appeal - 25%
  • Sincerity - 25%

In the event of a tie, duplicate prizes will be awarded. Decisions of the judges are final.

Prize: A 6-night/7-day stay for two at the Inter-Continental San Juan Resort & Casino, including round-trip coach air transportation from gateway airport nearest winner's home (approximate retail value: $4,000). Prize includes breakfast daily and a mother and daughter day of beauty at the beachfront hotel's spa. Prize consists of only those items listed as part of the prize. Prize is valued in U.S. currency.

All entries become the property of Torstar Corp. and will not be returned. No responsibility is assumed for lost, late, illegible, incomplete, inaccurate, non-delivered or misdirected mail or misdirected e-mail, for technical, hardware or software failures of any kind, lost or unavailable network connections, or failed, incomplete, garbled or delayed computer transmission or any human error which may occur in the receipt or processing of the entries in this Contest.

Contest open only to residents of the U.S. (except Colorado) and Canada, who are 18 years of age or older and is void wherever prohibited by law; all applicable laws and regulations apply. Any litigation within the Province of Quebec respecting the conduct or organization of a publicity contest may be submitted to the Régie des alcools, des courses et des jeux for a ruling. Any litigation respecting the awarding of a prize may be submitted to the Régie des alcools, des courses et des jeux only for the purpose of helping the parties reach a settlement. Employees and immediate family members of Torstar Corp. and D.L. Blair, Inc., their affiliates, subsidiaries and all other agencies, entities and persons connected with the use, marketing or conduct of this Contest are not eligible to enter. Taxes on prize are the sole responsibility of winner. Acceptance of any prize offered constitutes permission to use winner's name, photograph or other likeness for the purposes of advertising, trade and promotion on behalf of Torstar Corp., its affiliates and subsidiaries without further compensation to the winner, unless prohibited by law.

Winner will be determined no later than April 15, 2002 and be notified by mail. Winner will be required to sign and return an Affidavit of Eligibility form within 15 days after winner notification. Non-compliance within that time period may result in disqualification and an alternate winner may be selected. Winner of trip must execute a Release of Liability prior to ticketing and must possess required travel documents (e.g. Passport, photo ID) where applicable. Travel must be completed within 12 months of selection and is subject to traveling companion completing and returning a Release of Liability prior to travel; and hotel and flight accommodations availability. Certain restrictions and blackout dates may apply. No substitution of prize permitted by winner. Torstar Corp. and D.L. Blair, Inc., their parents, affiliates, and subsidiaries are not responsible for errors in printing or electronic presentation of Contest, or entries. In the event of printing or other errors which may result in unintended prize values or duplication of prizes, all affected entries shall be null and void. If for any reason the Internet portion of the Contest is not capable of running as planned, including infection by computer virus, bugs, tampering, unauthorized intervention, fraud, technical failures, or any other causes beyond the control of Torstar Corp. which corrupt or affect the administration, secrecy, fairness, integrity or proper conduct of the Contest, Torstar Corp. reserves the right, at its sole discretion, to disqualify any individual who tampers with the entry process and to cancel, terminate, modify or suspend the Contest or the Internet portion thereof. In the event the Internet portion must be terminated a notice will be posted on the website and all entries received prior to termination will be judged in accordance with these rules. In the event of a dispute regarding an on-line entry, the entry will be deemed submitted by the authorized holder of the e-mail account submitted at the time of entry. Authorized account holder is defined as the natural person who is assigned to an e-mail address by an Internet access provider, on-line service provider or other organization that is responsible for arranging e-mail address for the domain associated with the submitted e-mail address. Torstar Corp. and/or D.L. Blair Inc. assumes no responsibility for any computer injury or damage related to or resulting from accessing and/or downloading any sweepstakes material. Rules are subject to any requirements/limitations imposed by the FCC. Purchase or acceptance of a product offer does not improve your chances of winning.

For winner's name (available after May 1, 2002), send a self-addressed, stamped envelope to: Harlequin Mother's Day Contest Winners 2216, P.O. Box 4200 Blair, NE 68009-4200 or you may access the www.eHarlequin.com Web site through June 3, 2002.

Contest sponsored by Torstar Corp., P.O. Box 9042, Buffalo, NY 14269-9042.

If you enjoyed what you just read,
then we've got an offer you can't resist!

Take 2 bestselling
love stories FREE!
Plus get a FREE surprise gift!